THE BILLIONAIRE'S POSSESSION

BRI BLACKWOOD

BRETAGEY PRESS

NOTE FROM THE AUTHOR

Hello!

Thank you for taking the time to read this book. The Billionaire's Possession is a dark billionaire enemies-to-lovers romance. It is not recommended for minors and contains situations that are dubious and could be triggering. The book also includes sexual assault and flashbacks to child abuse which might also be triggering. It isn't a standalone and the book ends in a cliffhanger. The next book in the series is The Billionaire's Vengeance.

Chapter 13 contains graphic violence and blood.

BLURB

I could run, but I couldn't hide.

If there's one thing I learned in this life, is that I couldn't stay where I'm not wanted.

That's why I fled from Ace Bolton's home and went into hiding.

No one would care if I was gone or so I thought.

Staying hidden while the world around me imploded was the only way I thought I could stay safe.

But nothing is ever as it seems.

When danger comes knocking on my doorstep, it sends me running.

Right back into the arms of my monster.

PLAYLIST

Teeth - 5 Seconds of Summer
Ain't No Rest for the Wicked - Cage The Elephant
Let's Kill Tonight - Panic! At The Disco
Bloody Mary - Lady Gaga
Don't Blame Me - Taylor Swift
The Hills - The Weeknd
You Made Me Do It - Tommee Profitt, Ruby Amanfu
Stargirl Interlude - The Weeknd, Lana Del Rey
Immortals - Fall Out Boy

The playlist can be found on Spotify.

1

HARLOW

No matter what I did, I couldn't stop my lip from quivering. The events over the last month or so played out before me like a movie in my head. What the hell was all of this?

"I'm fucked, aren't I?"

That's all I could think to say as the wind blew through my hair. Except I wasn't driving. I wasn't in Ace's BMW cruising down the street to Beyond the Page. I was sitting in the passenger seat of Emma's old car, driving to who knew where.

Tears flowed down my face. Wiping them away felt like a chore I couldn't perform. My self-control was hanging by a thread. I wanted to pound my fists into something but hurting myself by trying to hit something in Emma's car wasn't wise.

No matter how much I willed myself to stop crying, I couldn't. The activities over the last few weeks had taken their toll and now I was reaping the benefits. A part of my heart felt as if it were still at Ace's home. I missed being with him, something I hadn't expected to feel the night he'd driven me to his home and declared that he was going to get all of his money's worth from me. Yet here I was upset that he'd rejected me, and it led to me fleeing his home with a friend in her getaway car.

And the tinge of regret in the pit of my stomach? It was growing larger as the miles between me and Ace grew. What had I done? The question played on repeat in my mind, but every conclusion I reached was the same. If given the chance, I would do the same thing again.

I knew this stemmed from never feeling like I truly belonged anywhere. While there had been moments of stability in my life, most of the time, I felt as if I was in constant states of upheaval. This was no different.

With a heavy sigh, I finally wiped the tears and glanced at Emma. She and I stayed silent since we'd left Brentson, and I attributed that mostly to me being in shock. I'd pulled this off with no problems other than being an emotional wreck.

"You're not. This is a fucked-up situation, but you aren't fucked, Harlow."

It was weird to be on the other side of this conversation. Usually, it was me talking Emma down and now the tables had turned.

"Where are we going?"

She glanced at me out of the corner of her eye. "I got you a place to stay for a while."

I pushed my hair behind my ears as I thought about what she said. This seemed too good to be true. "Is there a catch?"

"Of course not. Why would you think that?"

"After what I've just been through, you can never be too sure."

"Good point, but this one has no strings attached. I paid the first month's rent for you."

My mouth dropped open. Where the hell had she gotten the money? It would be rude to ask. "You didn't have to do that."

"It was no biggie. I had a bit more money this month and was happy to do it, but you'll have to cover next month's rent if you're still there."

I nodded. There was still some money in a savings account that might carry me for a couple of months if I was thrifty enough. I needed to find a job, and fast.

"We need to stop somewhere so I can buy a phone."

"Got you covered. Same brand as your old one. It's in the back seat."

I raised an eyebrow at her. "You really thought of everything."

"I tried. I wanted to make sure you had nothing to worry about here. I know you would do the same if I was in this situation."

She was right. I would make sure that she had everything she needed to survive. And she was helping me with that first step. I didn't know if I could ever repay her.

"How much is the room?"

"Four hundred a month. And it's not too far from the city."

Not bad, especially if it was close to New York City. Things were going to be okay, or so I told myself. Because that was the only thing I could hold on to.

We cruised down the interstate and she turned off at an exit labeled Dalhurst. I'd never heard of it, but that meant little since New York State was big and I hadn't heard of Brentson until I drove there in Ace's car.

Before I could ask, Emma said, "The place I found for you is in this town."

"Dalhurst..." I mumbled before I said, "How did you organize all of this so fast?"

"I know someone who grew up here and her family has several rental properties. We were lucky that the current tenants were looking for someone else to move in to help them pay the rent."

Yes, I was lucky. I didn't feel lucky at this very moment, but deep down I knew I was.

"Before I take you to your new place, we should pick up any essentials you might need."

I nodded. "I'll definitely need to get some food."

I rubbed my hands over my face and sighed. There was so much I needed to do whenever I got to Dalhurst. One of the biggest priorities was finding a job, hopefully something I could do remotely.

"Everything is going to work out, Harlow. I promise."

"Doesn't seem like it right now," I mumbled. The farther we drove away from Brentson, the more my heart continued to break. The urge to ask Emma to turn around and go back to Ace's home was there, but I knew I couldn't.

"Listen, I couldn't grab everything that you might need, but I was able to get something that might help you for the time being. It's in the back seat too."

This time, I glanced at her before looking in the back seat again. There sat a small black duffel bag. Thoughts about what could be in there clouded my mind until my brain settled on what I thought it could be. I turned to look back at Emma. "What did you do?"

"I didn't do anything. Look inside."

The hairs on the back of my neck stood at attention as I twisted my body to grab the bag. With a loud grunt, I pulled the bag into my lap and glanced at Emma.

"Open it," she said confidently.

I felt anything but. My hand shook slightly as I pulled the zipper, bracing myself for what I might find. When I finally opened the duffel, I looked inside and gasped.

"What the hell did you do?"

There were stacks of money in the bag, more money than I'd ever seen in my life.

"Falcone owed me some money and I decided to collect."

"Are you crazy? If he knows what you did, he's going to come after you! Not only do you owe him money, but you've also now stolen from him."

Based on the amount of money in the bag, there was no way he didn't know that this was missing. Given how closely he monitored those that owed him money, he had to know someone had stolen from him. And with Emma not being there...

Emma shrugged. "I'm not worried about Falcone. He has bigger concerns than me right now."

I closed my eyes as a dull headache formed. "This isn't making any sense."

"Falcone has bigger problems to deal with right now because the Mafia is after him. Trust me when I say, he's distracted, and I took it as an opportunity to snatch what I could and get out."

"But Emma—"

"Take what you need. Think of it as karma for Falcone. At least, that's how I'm viewing it."

I didn't feel comfortable taking money that wasn't my own. But it was from Falcone, and he could take a deep dive into hell for all I cared. And I needed the money to give myself some more wiggle room and paying in cash right now would help me maintain some anonymity.

I flipped through one stack and watched as the hundred-dollar bills and twenty-dollar bills flashed before my eyes. Before I could second-guess myself, I took three stacks and stashed them in my bag. I zipped the duffel bag back up and tossed it into the back seat. Out of sight, out of mind.

"And you're sure he won't notice this is gone? The last thing I want is for him to come after you."

Emma glanced at me out of the corner of her eye. "When I tell you the Mafia has Falcone spinning in circles around Bar 53, I mean it. All of his focus has been on making sure he can build up his guys to fight what might end up being an all-out war. Even Ian has been missing in action."

"But why is the Mafia after Falcone?"

"Your guess is as good as mine. I only know what I know based on bits and pieces that I heard and snatched this bag when I was given the chance. You know what I know."

Shit. Being in the dark was a disadvantage for sure, something that I needed to overcome. My mind drifted back to the other elephant in the room. Although I've tried to keep my mind off of him, it needed to be addressed.

"Do you know where Ian is?"

Dread filled me before I could finish the question. If Falcone was so worried about the Mafia then Ian probably was too. Then again, I'd only seen Ian managing Bar 53, so why would he be involved in this?

"Not sure," Emma said. "All I know is that he hadn't been around much before I left."

That didn't ease my dread. There was always going to be a downside to leaving the safety net that being with Ace provided. But it was so much more than that. The warmth that would course through my body as his gaze studied me was enough to set my soul ablaze.

I shook my head to rid my thoughts of Ace and found myself thinking back to Falcone and Ian. I was a sitting duck if either of them wanted to come after me and I knew that at least one of them was hell-bent on revenge because he didn't get what he wanted.

Emma cleared her throat, drawing my attention to her. "We're almost there now."

2

HARLOW

I knew how to disappear. It was something I had perfected once I'd aged out of foster care. Those skills came in handy now as I got settled into the room Emma was able to rent for me on short notice.

It wasn't much, but it was a roof over my head for the time being. But I needed to come up with a plan fast. I was lucky enough to find a bedroom that was my own, but I shared a bathroom with another woman across the hall and the kitchen with the other people in the home. I'd been here only a couple of days, so I'd met only one of my housemates.

Thankfully, the bedroom had come with the basics, like a bed and a dresser. I'd tried to make it my own by adding some personal touches. Putting up a photo of me and Mama Robinson on the dresser helped brighten the space for me. The room was nothing to write home about, but I couldn't complain. After all, I still had a bed to sleep in, and I wasn't in immediate danger. Or so I told myself, to keep my panicked nerves at bay.

In the back of my mind, I had no doubts that Ace would

betray me because he had no use for me anymore. If I didn't have a target on my back right now, it was only a matter of time.

I picked up the cheap phone Emma brought me. There was only one person who knew this number.

"Hi, Emma."

"Hey, listen, I can't talk long but I needed to tell you th—this."

The stuttering in her voice made me pause. I'd been worried that this whole mission to get me out of Ace's clutches might prove to be too much for her. And knowing that she stole from Falcone was a bigger problem. All of this combined made me worried that I was right.

"What's wrong?"

"I won't be coming around for a while because I don't want Falcone to know that I know where you are."

Hearing Falcone's name made my heart sink. I wondered if he would come after me next, but I wasn't surprised. After all, I had expected Ace to tell Falcone that I didn't honor our deal and demand his money back. Then again, Ace could be searching for me, too.

I didn't trust him. I left because it was easy to see that he didn't trust me either. Nothing that had developed after the auction meant anything to him. The desire for more and to be treated better won.

"Thanks for telling me. I guess all I can do is keep an eye out for Falcone, because we know that he'll be paying me a visit."

Because I knew it wasn't a matter of if, it was a matter of when.

"How is life on the outside?" I hadn't stepped foot outside

of this new place I called home since I arrived, for fear of getting spotted by Ace. In the back of my mind, Falcone was also on the list of people after me. Now they both sat side by side on the mental note I'd constructed in my brain.

Who was more dangerous?

Well, only one of them had threatened to kill me. But Ace had scared me more than anyone could have.

He'd wrecked my thoughts and my body and made me wonder what a happily ever after between us would look like. And now the only salvation I had was this sparsely furnished room.

Emma snorted. "How can you joke at a time like this?"

I was so caught up in my thoughts that I briefly forgot what we were talking about.

"It's the only thing that's keeping me going, if I'm being honest."

"Understandable. Do you want me to grab some groceries for you? I didn't leave you much. A quick order pickup won't take too long."

I had enough food to get by for the next day or so, but I was going to have to buy some.

"No, because just in case Falcone has eyes on you... it might not be the wisest idea."

I sighed. "I'm sorry for getting you into this situation."

"You shouldn't be because you don't have anything to be sorry for. I said I would help you and I will."

I smiled at her declaration. "I'm so happy to have you in my life."

"And I appreciate all that you've done for me, especially with Ian."

I groaned. I hadn't thought about him in days, and now

all my memories of him came rushing back. My hand reached for my neck to touch the bruise that was now gone. I could sometimes still feel his hand around my throat.

"You don't have to worry about me when it comes to him anymore. Look, I need to go. I'll be in touch soon, okay?"

"Talk to you soon."

With that, we both hung up, and once again, I was alone. And being alone meant that I only had time to dwell on the situation I was in.

At least I had some of my books to distract me from this horrible world. I longed to go back to a bookstore and get lost in a world that only my imagination and the words of others could create. Maybe in a few days when I had enough nerve to leave the house, outside of going to the grocery store, I could see if there was a library or bookshop nearby. I picked up one of my older books, one that I've had for a few years and that I've read a million times as evidenced by the wear and tear. It sat next to the photo of Mama Robinson that I brought with me everywhere.

A tear fell from my eye before I realized I'd started crying. My mouth trembled as I tried to hold it all together but failed. Instead of continuing to fight it, I gave in to the sadness I felt at having my world ripped apart for the second time in about a month.

Yes, I'd been the one to leave the safety that Ace's home brought, but I couldn't stay where I wasn't wanted. Deep down, I'd wanted him to say anything except effectively ending... whatever it is we had. Would I have been prepared for him to declare his undying love for me instead? No. But I didn't know he would turn his back on this thing we had.

In hindsight, it might have been foolish to leave, but there was always a chance that Falcone might change his mind and come after me, even if the deal with Ace had been fulfilled. So, I took matters into my own hands, not knowing where it might lead me.

It led me here, weeping in a bedroom that wasn't my own, wondering if I'd made a huge mistake. Deep down, I knew I hadn't because I needed to prove to myself that I was worth it. There wasn't much I could do to take it back now, so why was I still crying?

I tried to keep as quiet as possible. I didn't need the ears of strangers knowing that I was crying or showing a sign of weakness because there was always the risk of someone trying to get the upper hand. It was important for me to always be on my guard because you never knew what was going to come and slap you in the face. And sometimes, when you knew it was coming, you still didn't feel prepared.

I wiped away the tears, hoping to convince myself that I had nothing to cry about. I'd made my choice, had an idea of what I was getting into, and still felt as if I was a complete failure.

With one final sniffle, I pushed my shoulders back and took a deep breath.

You will get through this. You will get through this.

3

ACE

The darkness of my office mirrored what my mind felt like. But there was something else there. A thrashing in my head that had nothing to do with a headache. It was from the rage that I tried to keep buried. I'd done my best to keep my emotions under control, but I'd failed.

I slammed my left fist down on my desk before I snatched the closest thing I could grab with my right. Before I could stop myself, I threw the mug and watched it crash into the wall, shattering into pieces. Did my throwing it solve anything? No, but it felt damn good to let some of my pent-up aggression out.

Staring at the mess that I made, I found it poetic in a way. The mug was a perfect reflection of me. I was broken by circumstances beyond my control. While I couldn't have stopped the abuse I received from Kiki Hastings, I knew that I could have prevented the situation I was currently in with Harlow.

I knew I didn't deserve her, and the thought burned through me like a bomb detonating. She should have someone who could give her everything she ever wanted or needed. There was no way she could get that with me. That further fed into the anger I felt. This whole situation was a shit show, and I shouldn't have taken Kingston up on this opportunity to help Will DePalma.

But then I would have never met Harlow. The woman who had made me feel things I'd never felt and turned my world upside down. And now she was an easy target for anyone who wanted to get back at me.

I bent down to get a better look at the mug. On the bright side, at least I was smart enough to throw a mug that didn't have any liquid in it.

"I can help you clean it up, sir."

I found Anderson standing in the doorway of my office. His normally stoic facial expression had changed slightly. His eyes had widened, and I knew why. In the time that I'd moved in, he'd never seen me lose my temper, because I usually didn't. Focusing on the logical options in a situation helped me shove any emotion to the curb, but that wasn't the case.

"Don't worry. I got it."

"Is there anything I can get you?"

I shook my head, wanting him to leave as quickly as possible so that I could be alone with my thoughts. When he'd finally done so, it was then that I allowed myself to move from behind my desk and toward the mess that I'd made.

Thoughts of Harlow consumed me, more than I cared to admit. Her blonde hair wrapped around my fingers. The sight of her lush lips begging to be kissed but knowing I couldn't. Her love for reading and the evenings that I would find her in my library, her head deep into a book that she'd picked up.

But most of all, I missed her, and it had nothing to do with the arrangement we had or the money I'd forked over to buy her at Falcone's auction. Fuck the money. I wanted her even when I shouldn't.

It took some time for me to admit to myself that I'd been an idiot when I pushed her away, but I'd thought she would take me up on my offer to still stay here until the end of our arrangement. Obviously, I was wrong, and I was glad I'd had the foresight to take precautions to protect what was mine. It was all under the guise of a gift.

The bracelet served as a piece of jewelry for her, but it doubled as a way to keep tabs on her location when necessary. I hadn't felt the need to use it when she was in my home, but since she'd been gone, all bets were off.

My plan to protect Harlow had failed. The tracker I'd had installed in the bracelet wasn't displaying a signal that could pinpoint where she was.

As of this moment, she'd disappeared without a trace, but there were a couple of leads we were following up on. Through Cross Sentinel, the security company that Kingston had founded, we were trying to track down both Harlow and Emma. I thought that finding Emma would mean we would have an easier time finding Harlow. Emma might also end up telling on herself and lead us to exactly what she was doing working at one of Falcone's establishments, when she didn't owe him a cent.

What was her role in all of this outside of helping Harlow

get away? Chanel had confirmed that there was a brunette driving the car that had picked up Harlow, but that was the most she could see from her shop. She didn't catch much of the car outside of figuring it was black or navy blue. She'd felt sorry that she hadn't been able to provide more information and asked if it was worth calling the police. I declined because it wasn't. The police wouldn't be helpful here, and it would be smart if Harlow didn't involve them either.

Bringing the police into this situation would complicate matters significantly, and depending on where she was, it could make it easier for me to track her down. But it would also make it easier for Falcone and his men as well.

I bent down to pick up the shards when my cell phone rang. I paused for a moment, wondering if it was worth stopping my current task before it clicked that it might be an important call. It was a good thing that I picked up because it turned out that Kingston was on the other end of the line.

"Ace, I told you I'd call as soon as I had some news."

"So, I assume this means you do?"

"Yes, and not the best kind."

I cursed and shut my eyes, steeling myself for what he was about to tell me. "What did you find out?"

"Not only has Harlow vanished, but so has Emma."

"You've got to be shitting me. I thought you said it wouldn't take you long to find her, so I could concentrate on finding Harlow. You promised you would bring her in for questioning."

Blaming Kingston for any of this was wrong, but I was too pissed off to care.

"I know, but we visited her last known address, and it was vacant. She wasn't at Bar 53 yesterday or today. That made us suspicious, so my team hacked into their scheduling system and found that she wasn't scheduled to come in for the next two weeks, at least. To disappear this fast requires resources. Based on what we know of her, we suspect someone is helping her to disappear."

"Maybe she's hiding with Harlow."

"Could be. I'm not sure if that's the smartest thing for them to do, however."

I preferred to act alone, so what Kingston said made sense to me. But if both women had no experience with being on the run, they might want to stick together. "Maybe Falcone is behind all of this? After all, we know Emma doesn't owe him any money."

"Potentially. Emma has worked there almost as long as Harlow, so Falcone could have brought her in to watch your girl."

"Harlow isn't connected to me outside of me buying her during an auction. Keep in mind that I was trying to gain intel on the case that you were supposed to handle."

"Denial is a hell of a drug."

"Watch yourself, Kingston. We might be associates, but I wouldn't hesitate to knock your fucking lights out."

Kingston snorted. "I'd love to see you try, my friend."

It was good to see that his smart-ass remarks were still alive and well. If only he knew what I would do to make sure that Harlow was safe.

A blinking light drew my attention to the computer screen. *Son of a bitch.*

"Kingston, I need to go. I'll call you in a few minutes."

"Wait—"

I hung up before I could hear another word. The mess on

the floor would have to wait. I'd call Kingston while I was in the car because there was no way I was missing this.

Here was the break in the case that we needed. The tracker I'd placed on the bracelet had turned on. It was time to bring Harlow back to where she belonged, which was with me.

4

ACE

With the night sky leading the way, I wasted no time in getting into my car and driving to the last place the tracker had shown the bracelet to be.

The apartment was located just outside of Brentson. I'd assumed that Harlow would be farther away by now, but apparently I was wrong. It would be relatively easy to get into the building, but it might prove difficult to find the exact unit that the bracelet was in. So I waited, hoping the bracelet would soon be on the move again.

This was the first stakeout I'd done since Harlow moved in with me. The last one I'd been on involved Kingston's secret half sister, and I'd volunteered to do it because of my proximity to Brentson University. I'd provided Kingston with everything that I'd found out, and it was up to him to decide what to do with that information.

Sitting here in silence, watching this apartment building, gave me a lot of time to think. Replaying the events that led to

Harlow's departure wasn't productive, but it was all I could do.

I knew that having her out of my life was the best option, but the void she'd left was indescribable. Having her on the outside, where anyone could get to her, had thrown me off because my only objective had been to get her away from me as fast as possible.

That had been easy to do, but I knew it had been the wrong choice for her safety. My logical thinking had been thrown out the window. In an effort to get her away from me, I hadn't thought about all the possibilities that could have arisen due to her being close to me. That had been an error on my part. I didn't like to admit that she had somehow gotten under my skin and now someone could use that to their advantage. Falcone and his minion were the first ones to come to mind since he knew the real reason why I was meeting with him and attending the auction.

Thinking back to the auction, I'd assumed that her not having to fulfill one of the primary obligations that we set forth in our agreement would have made her happy, but the opposite happened. The rejection in her eyes was palpable and should have been a hint that she would do something drastic.

But it didn't occur to me. I thought that the fear of what Falcone might do to her if I took back the million dollars I'd spent would be enough to bind her to me.

But I was wrong.

It was a rare mistake I'd made, and now I had to deal with the consequences. I was determined to right this wrong, and every second that ticked by without an alert from this tracker further fueled the fire that burned deep inside of me.

I glanced to my right when I heard a sound that wasn't the one I was expecting. My phone, which was connected to my car's Bluetooth, rang. I glared at the intrusion and then my eyes narrowed when I saw who was calling. Instead of answering, I declined the call. I would deal with that issue later.

As if I'd voiced my frustrations out loud and the tracker had heard me, the small dot that represented the bracelet began to move. A hooded figure exited the apartment building, and even with the baggy clothes, I figured it was more than likely a man that was of medium height and build. He was glancing around as if he was suspicious that someone might be looking for him.

Too bad that the person looking for him was me.

His paranoia didn't end there. He walked about ten feet before he looked around again, giving me extra time to confirm that it was indeed him who was making the tracker move. When he turned back around, I exited my car, and my longer stride ate up the distance between us. I didn't even bother locking my car doors because I knew that this would be quick.

He saw me coming at the last moment, but before he could react, I'd covered his mouth and threw him up against the wall, not giving a shit who might come by and see our interaction.

"If you don't want to die, you'll answer the questions that I have for you. Got it?"

When he nodded, I removed my hand.

"What the fuck, dude!" he exclaimed as his eyes shifted between me and the quiet street that we were on. His movements were jerky, and when he tried to focus on me, his eyes appeared to glaze over.

He was on something, but I didn't have time to find out what.

"What's your name?"

"Who the hell wants to know?"

The glare I sent him had him changing his tune.

"It's S-Shorty."

I was confident that 'Shorty' wasn't his real name, but that didn't matter because it wouldn't be hard for me or Kingston to track him and his associates down. I searched his pockets, and it didn't take me long to locate a slender, circular object. It could only be one thing. When I pulled my hand out of his coat pocket, I shoved the item into his face.

"Who gave you this bracelet?" It was the one I'd given to Harlow. How was she connected to this fucker?

"Uh—"

"Tell me right now."

"I got it in an exchange."

"In an exchange for what? Who was the person that you did the exchange with?"

"Look, dude, I promised I wouldn't say anything. I'm running a business here and I have to keep my connections quiet."

"Hey, dude, if you don't start talking, I have no problem putting an end to this right here." I placed the bracelet in my pocket before opening my coat and revealing the gun in my holster.

Shorty's eyes widened slightly, and he again looked up and down the street before he turned back to me and whispered, "I don't want any trouble."

"And there will be none if you tell me what I want to know."

He sighed loudly. "Fine. I got it in a trade for drugs because I gave her some and she gave this to me in return. Bitch was supposed to pay me and instead I got this. I was headed to the pawnshop in the morning to see what I could get for it."

"Funny that won't be happening now."

"Oh, come on—"

"Who gave you the bracelet?"

"Um..." His voice trailed off as his eyes shot to the sky. He'd better be trying to recall who the person was and not making up a lie on the fly.

"Her name was... Hanna, maybe?"

I watched as his eyes wandered around, looking everywhere but me. "You're going to have to do better than that, maybe." If he'd fucked up the name, he could be referring to either Harlow or Emma.

"She was a small brunette and—"

Definitely not Harlow then. "Was her name Emma?"

"That's it! That's her name. How did you know?"

"Lucky guess. When was the last time you saw her?"

"Yesterday... or maybe the day before? What is time?"

I could imagine that time would be an odd concept to someone who might not abide by it. However, I'd been fixated on time. Harlow left my home about a week ago, so who knows when he actually met up with Emma.

"How did you connect with her?"

"Huh?"

I rolled my eyes, losing the last bit of patience that I had. "How did you arrange the drop?"

"Phone. Can I reach into my pocket and grab my phone?"

I raised an eyebrow at him. If he thought I trusted him not to pull a fast one, he had another thing coming. "I can get it. Which pocket?"

"Back left."

I maneuvered my arm so that I could snatch the phone out of his pocket. "Give me the number."

"Okay, but I'm going to need my arm back."

I eyed him before taking a step back, giving him the ability to look at his phone. I too took out my phone, ready to type in the number.

"555-555-0046."

I added the number to my contacts and then pulled out a business card that only had the number to one of the phones that I used when conducting business such as this.

"If she contacts you again, you call this number. Got it?"

He nodded and I backed away from him. As I was turning to walk back to my car, I heard him mumble something under his breath.

"About time you got off of me, you stupid son of a—"

Without another thought, I threw a punch that landed on his face. Almost immediately, his body slid down the wall into a sitting position. I checked for a pulse before I placed a couple of hundred-dollar bills in his coat. Hopefully, they would be there when he came to.

Was Harlow somewhere in this area? It would take hours and a lot of manpower to cover all the towns between my home, Brentson, and New York City, and that was if she was still in the state.

My phone rang, and I glanced at my dashboard to see

who was calling. When the name appeared, I sent the call to voicemail before pulling away from the curb.

5

HARLOW

A knock on my bedroom door made my heart skip a beat. Who could that be?

I hadn't been here long and didn't say anything to anyone outside of hello or goodbye. So what gives?

Instead of continuing to run through the million and a half possibilities that this knock could mean, I walked over to the door and opened it before I could talk myself out of it. A petite redhead was standing on the other side.

What was her name again? Clara... Chelsea....

"Hey, I was about to go to the grocery store. I know you're new here, so do you want to come with?"

Chloe. That was her name as I recalled her introduction when I arrived. I crossed my arms over my sweatshirt, unsure about the interaction. The woman in front of me rolled her eyes and shook her head.

"I'm so bad at this, I apologize. Just trying to be friendly, I guess. I noticed you didn't have a car from what I could see, so I figured I would ask if you wanted to go to the store to pick up some things. I have a car and was going to make a run myself."

Her offer seemed reasonable enough, and I needed to go to pick up some groceries. But I was suspicious.

"I'm Sam." That was the first name I could think of off the top of my head.

"Well, it's nice to meet you. Do you want to head out now?"

"I didn't say I was going to begin with."

This time, Chloe slapped a hand on her forehead and said, "There I go again. Would you like to come to the store?"

Her offer was generous, and she seemed nice enough, so what was the harm? Plus, I'd given her a fake name.

"Yes. Yes I would."

She clapped her hands together. "Excellent! How about we leave in about ten minutes? Is that enough time for you?"

"That's plenty of time. Thanks for offering to take me."

Chloe shrugged. "It's not a problem at all. I'll meet you at the front door in ten."

She left me to stare at the empty space she'd left. I closed the door and walked back into the room to gather the things I needed for the store. With a baseball cap on my head and sunglasses shielding my eyes, I was ready to go. I walked into the bathroom to pull myself together a bit more and locked the door behind me. Living in a house with a bunch of strangers would take some getting used to and I had to be even more careful because of the money that Emma had given to me. If it wasn't safe, buried deep in the back of my closet and behind a locked door then I was screwed. Instead of dwelling on it further, I walked downstairs and found Chloe at the door.

"Are you ready to go?" she asked when I reached the landing.

I nodded, and we walked in silence to the parking lot where she led me to an older bright-red Honda. The car was in better shape than my car. I wondered what condition my car was in since I hadn't seen it in well over a month. Maybe I could ask Emma to do me a favor?

"So what brought you to Dalhurst? It's strange to have a newcomer around here."

"Why is that?" I asked a question to avoid having to answer hers.

"Most people that live here have lived here their whole lives. So, either you stay here until you die, or you get out and never return, which is why I'm curious about how you got here."

"That's interesting. Didn't realize that when I started renting my room."

"Yeah, so what's your story?"

Chloe wouldn't let up. Since I was stuck in her car with her, I had to answer the question. "I needed to get away for a while. Figure out what I'm doing with my life." It was a bit more in depth than that, but I thought it was a nice synopsis.

"Ah, same for me. I think I'm going to head to New York City soon. I've always wanted to live there."

Her words tugged at my heartstrings. I missed what life was like with Mama Robinson before my life went straight to shit.

"New York City is an interesting place." My response wasn't a lie.

Chloe looked at me and grinned. "I know. Even more reason to visit or live there for a time."

I shrugged. She had a good point, and it was a bucket list item for many. In a way, I longed to be back in familiar territory. But what would NYC offer me when I returned? The question stayed with me as Chloe drove us to the grocery store. When we arrived, we exited the car and grabbed handheld baskets.

"Want to meet at the cash registers in about twenty-five minutes?"

I nodded, happy that I didn't have to make awkward conversation with her while we shopped. She gave me a small smile before she walked away, and I turned and headed in the opposite direction.

I strolled up and down the aisles aimlessly, trying to find food that would be easy for me to throw together that wasn't expensive. After all, I was only fixing food for one. Yes, my housemates were strangers, but I hoped that there would be some common decency between us all that would prevent any of my things from being stolen. I continued wandering around the store and picked up some basics that would get me through at least the next few days.

I lowered my sunglasses and found myself in the hair products aisle, staring at different hair dyes. I set my basket at my feet and studied several of the boxes, debating whether I wanted to dye my hair, and if so, which color.

Suddenly, an eerie feeling came over me, as if I was being watched. I looked up from the boxes of hair dye and glanced to my left and to my right. There was nothing there. Confirming that no one was in the aisle didn't help the goose bumps that appeared on my skin. I pulled my baseball cap lower and turned my attention back to the dye.

A light brown wouldn't be a bad idea, and it would be

closer to matching my roots. Before I could talk myself out of it, I tossed the box of dye into the basket and moved on. I grabbed a couple more things before I ended up at the cashiers. Chloe called my name just as I was about to pay for my groceries. When I had my items in hand, Chloe and I walked out of the store and back to her car.

"Did you find everything you needed?"

I had and then some. "Yes. I also bought some hair dye."

Chloe's eyes widened before she popped open the trunk of her car. "Thinking of changing things up?"

"Something like that. New place to live, new hair? Who knows what else I might do?"

Chloe chuckled. "Well, if you need any help, let me know. I'd be happy to."

"Sounds like a plan." I couldn't help but smile, and it was the first time since leaving Ace's home that I felt the desire to do so.

After Chloe left, I spent the rest of the evening in my bedroom and soon I lay in bed, wishing that sleep would come sooner rather than later.

THE LIGHT FEATHERY touches that danced along my skin soon turned rough. The dramatic change in pressure forced my eyes awake as I tried to figure out what was going on.

There I saw Ace standing over me and a gasp left my throat. What was he doing here?

"Sweetness," Ace said. His voice was so deep that I almost couldn't make out what he said. But his term of endearment called out to me like a magnet, drawing me into him.

"I'm going to play with this beautiful body of yours and only when I say you can come will you do so. Do you understand?"

All I could do was nod my head because I was at a loss for words. What the hell was going on here?

He wasted no time in pulling up my T-shirt and attacking my bare breasts with his mouth, alternating between licking, sucking, and gently biting my nipple. His other hand kept my other breast entertained. I leaned into his touch, wishing that he would never stop the assault on my tits.

When one of my breasts fell out of his mouth with a soft pop, he said, "You're not allowed to touch your pussy until I say you can."

I hadn't even realized my hand had moved. I nodded, happy to give him whatever he wanted, as long as he didn't stop touching me.

"Fuck, baby," he said as he moved his face to my other breast, determined to give it the same attention. One of his hands made its way down my body, lightly brushing against my inner thigh and making me silently wish that he would use his fingers to fuck me.

He continued to tease me while I wiggled underneath him. As if he could sense my desperation, he inserted one finger into my pussy, and I sighed in relief. My eyes closed as I enjoyed the sensation of him fucking me with his hand and when I opened my eyes, I found his dark orbs staring back at me. His pace increased and soon I felt him add a second finger to the mix.

"That's it, sweetness. Show me how much you like my fingers in this sweet pussy."

A groan left my lips. It seemed as if words escaped me, yet he knew every move I craved and how much I wanted him. My body had a mind of its own and began to ride his hand.

When his fingers were fucking me at a rapid pace, I couldn't *keep up with the sensations it was making me feel. I knew there was a good chance that I could explode all over his hand and that he wouldn't mind that one bit.*

"Are you getting close, Harlow?"

My name falling off his lips was sexy as fuck. I nodded again and sucked in a deep breath as I felt myself crossing the point of no return.

"You're going to come for me... right now."

THAT WAS the last thing I heard him say. I woke up with a racing heart and was disappointed to find myself all alone. How had that dream been so powerful that everything in it felt real? My hand made its way down to my pussy, where I found myself dripping wet from the events that unfolded in my dream. Even in sleep, my body felt as if it belonged to Ace.

There was no way in hell I was going to let my arousal go to waste. My hand softly touched my clit before increasing the pressure and speed. I continued what the dream had started, feeling the power within my body build and build until I was on the edge of exploding. The image of Ace looking down at me while he brought me to my climax was at the forefront of my mind.

I stripped the covers from my body, tossed a sweatshirt over the tank top and shorts I'd worn to bed and walked into the bathroom. By the time I reached the sink, I realized I'd forgotten to lock my door, but I refused to go back. I didn't hear anyone else wandering about and it would only take me a second to do what I wanted to do. I splashed some cool water on my face in an attempt to rid my memory of the dream. Of course, it didn't work, and I thought about it more. Dissecting every move, wishing that I could reenact it with him right here, right now.

It wasn't logical to have sex dreams about someone who rejected you. To long for their touch when the other person wanted nothing to do with you.

6

ACE

I stared at the piece of paper with the last known number for Emma, thinking that it would be better served as kindling for my fireplace. I'd called the phone number multiple times to confirm that it indeed went directly to voicemail. It wouldn't be a surprise if Emma had connected the number to a burner phone she'd discarded, meaning that I was back at square one. Just in case, I'd done my research to see if I could find any information about the number. I'd also sent it and anything I was able to find to Kingston for him and his team to do their due diligence as well. It helped to have someone who had more manpower at their disposal to focus on this type of thing.

I should be working on what reports I want to tell my team we need to present to our board of directors, but I couldn't concentrate on it to save my life. The blinking cursor in my open document on my laptop openly mocked me for having been in the same position for too long.

I glanced up at the television that I turned on hours ago and something caught my eye. A brunette reporter was standing outside of a very familiar place. I grabbed the remote and turned the volume up.

"We're live in front of Bar 53, a popular restaurant in Midtown where there has been a shooting."

I mouthed the word 'fuck' to myself. Of course, this was outside of Bar 53. *Here we go.*

When the reporter opened her mouth to continue, my phone rang, and I assumed it was Kingston. I turned the television's volume down again and answered my phone.

"Ace," he said before I had a chance to say hello.

"What's wrong?" The tone of his voice told me something was up. Kingston was usually unflappable, but it was easy to detect the shakiness in his voice.

"Falcone and the Vitale crime family are fighting and it's only a matter of time before shit spills over."

I'd expected him to confirm the obvious. "I know. There was a short clip about it on the news."

The news didn't surprise me because I suspected it would happen at some point. With bloodshed starting to be carried out in the public sphere, along with news stories that weren't being buried, it didn't take much to connect the dots. If neither party were bothering to hide it anymore, this was getting messy.

Kingston's intel just before I found out that Harlow left was the only hint I needed. People talked and who knew who leaked the information. While I wanted to know who the rat was, I had more important things to worry about. Like the fact that my backup plan in case something like this had happened had failed.

I glared at the bracelet that I bought Harlow instead of responding to Kingston right away. It was as if the piece of jewelry was mocking me for thinking I was so clever. I couldn't help but wish I'd thought of locking her away from the world, much like I'd locked her in one of my guest rooms when she first arrived.

Or you could have just made her happy.

Deep down, I knew I couldn't, even if I wanted to.

Kingston's voice broke through my thoughts. "Are you still there?"

"I am." I paused before I continued. "If Falcone comes knocking at my door, it's going to be the worst mistake he's ever made. But I'm more concerned about Harlow. We both know that Falcone thinks that the way he can get to me is through her."

"I know and we're doing the best we can. I have my team working around the clock, trying to make sure that we get her back as quickly as possible. We're tracking down a couple of leads about Emma and hope to have news for you in a couple of hours."

Emma's name made me pause. "What leads are you tracking down about Emma?"

"The phone number led to nowhere, but we dug up some information on Emma. Her name is Emma Barlow, and she didn't exist until she started working with Falcone."

My eyes rolled up to the ceiling before I closed them. "This information shouldn't surprise me, but here I am. Why would Falcone go through lengths of concealing this woman's real identity?"

"We're tracking it down."

"Thanks. And if anything else comes up, call me as soon as possible."

"Of course."

I hung up the phone without saying another word and put it down on my desk. A quick look at the television showed that the news anchors had moved on to another story, so I wouldn't know what the afternoon news reported about the shooting outside of Bar 53 unless I did my own research online or made some phone calls.

I didn't give a fuck about myself because I didn't need anyone to protect me. My only concern was Harlow. I grabbed the piece of paper with Emma's number on it and walked over to my fireplace to toss it in.

Watching it burn was therapeutic. I walked back over to my desk, where I found the invitation from Falcone and the bracelet I'd given Harlow. I played with the bracelet, hoping that something would come to mind about what I could do to find her before Falcone.

If you had asked me a couple of years ago if I would be here, thinking about a woman who I'd known for less than two months, I would have said that you were a fucking liar. But here we were.

I grabbed my telephone and did a quick search on Bar 53. Four people were shot outside of the restaurant. Two had died, one was in stable condition and the other in critical. Based on what I'd read, they had released no names, but I was sure that if anyone that was involved had a connection to Harlow, Kingston would report it to me.

As I put my phone away, an idea came to me. I pocketed the bracelet and walked out of my office and stared at the bed Harlow slept in. Could there be something here that I missed? I'd told Anderson that under no circumstances was the room to be cleaned, and now I was thankful for that foresight.

I walked into the room and closed the door behind me, shutting out the outside world. The room seemed even darker than normal. I was pretty sure it was because Harlow wasn't standing in front of me, but something that reminded me of her was in the air.

The first thing that I smelled was the faint scent of her lavender shampoo that she loved so much, and instantly memories of me running my fingers through her hair appeared in my mind.

While Harlow had taken most of her possessions she'd brought to my house, there were still some things she'd left behind. That included the clothes I'd bought for her. Anderson had already mentioned it to me, but knowing what I knew of her, I wasn't surprised. She would second guess taking the things I'd bought her because she felt as if they weren't hers.

My phone ringing interrupted my thoughts. I pulled the phone out of my pocket and glanced down at the number. My eyes narrowed at the screen. I sent that call to voicemail again, because I wasn't prepared to deal with the shit-talking that would be on the other end of the line.

Instead, I focused on what she might have left here.

The cleaning people Anderson hired had listened and avoided cleaning anything. Not that there was much to clean because Harlow had kept the room neat when she stayed here.

My first stop was to check the drawers, and I found only a shirt that she must have left behind in her haste. Nothing was on the floor or underneath the bed. I walked over to the desk to see if anything was left. At one point, she'd had her laptop resting here, so she used this desk at least once.

The bathroom showed little promise and I stared at the partially empty containers of shampoo and conditioner that she'd left there. I picked up the bottle, untwisted the top, and allowed the smell that I associated with her to drift into the air.

It reminded me of how all of this could have been avoided if I hadn't been afraid. If I'd just gotten my shit together and let her in. I put the top back on and picked up both bottles. They belonged in the master suite with my things.

Before I left, I looked all around and found a sticky note that was stuck to the bottom of one of the drawers. There was an address on it and a quick search told me that it was for Lindow Cemetery in the city. Could she have headed back to New York City? Why did she write down this address?

I dropped her hair products into my bathroom and then took the piece of paper with me, walked down to my office, and typed the address into a browser. While I was looking through several websites, another idea popped up in my mind. Could this be related to her adoptive mother?

A quick search for her gravesite proved that Harlow had buried Cynthia Robinson at the cemetery listed on the Post-it Note. And her death anniversary was coming up. Was Harlow planning on visiting her grave for it?

It was a small lead, but a lead nonetheless, and one that I needed to investigate. If this was what would bring her back to me, then so be it.

7

HARLOW

Things were going well. In fact, it felt like things were going too well for me to be completely comfortable. That was usually what happened when you always suspected that things would take a turn for the worst.

Working from home was proving to be easier than I thought it would be. I'd found some freelance gigs that put some money in my pockets for essentials and allowed me to set aside a small amount for my savings. I was glad to be earning some money again. The money that I got from Emma still sat in a bag that I'd hidden deep in my closet, hoping no one would find it if someone were to search my room and that I would forget it existed. Only the former had happened so far, instead of the latter.

The only thing that could make this better was visiting Mama Robinson's gravesite because her death anniversary was coming up. I didn't like asking anyone for help normally, but I knew asking Chloe to borrow her car for a couple of hours would be worth it. It was a big ask for a practical stranger, but it wouldn't hurt to at least try. If she said no, I could bite the cost and hire a cab to take me to and from the cemetery.

I switched my browser tab and stretched my arms above my head, working out some of the kinks in my body. They'd formed as a result of sitting with my computer on my lap for too long. Working long hours meant more money and I needed as much as I could get. My eyes lazily skimmed the screen when something caught my eye. At some point, I'd opened a new window in my browser and was checking out different news sites. What made me freeze was this headline:

Four People Shot Outside Popular Restaurant in New York City

No. It couldn't be.

I tried to force my body to move, but I couldn't. This had to be a joke.

I read the entire article and sat back with my mouth agape. It was true. Holy shit, this really happened.

The shooting had taken place outside of Bar 53 and two of the four people died. Had someone I knew gotten hurt or killed?

I had no way of checking in with anyone outside of finding a way of getting in touch with Emma or going down to Bar 53 myself. That would mean that I was walking straight into Falcone's lion's den, so that wasn't an option.

My stomach growled, distracting me from the news article about the tragic event. That was when I checked the time and sighed. I'd skipped lunch in favor of continuing my tasks, so it was no wonder why I was starving. After the news I'd just read, it surprised me that I still had an appetite.

I closed my laptop, placed it on the bed, and walked downstairs to the kitchen. It wouldn't take much to throw together a sandwich and solve this issue. The only sound that could be heard as I walked through the house was my feet walking across the floor. All of my other housemates were out of the house during the workday, so I didn't have to worry about running into anyone in the common areas.

I was grateful to have the house to myself after the news I'd read. Having to explain why I was upset wasn't worth it, and I needed to keep my connection to Bar 53 a secret.

Thinking of Bar 53 made me relive my time there and the article I'd just read. I could feel tears forming in my eyes. *Now is not the time to cry, Harlow.*

I licked my lips before taking a deep breath to gather myself together. There was nothing I could do about it, and I didn't know if I knew anyone who'd been killed or injured. Maybe it was the fact that Mama Robinson's death anniversary was coming up that was making me more emotional than normal.

I tucked my hair behind my ears and pulled out the ingredients that I needed for a ham and cheese sandwich. It took almost no time to throw the meal together. When I was finished, I sat down at the small table in the room near a window and looked outside, enjoying this moment that I had to myself. Although there wasn't too much activity on the block this home was on, seeing people go about their daily lives made me long for such moments that I used to have.

It was a stark contrast to what was going on at my old job. I rubbed my eyes in order to relieve the tension that was forming inside of me. How I wished I had my old cell phone.

I pulled out my current cell phone and shook my head. While I was known to hang on to things until they broke, here I was with my third phone I'd had in about a month. I opened the flip phone and was shocked to see that I had an unread message.

Who the hell was this?

The message said I had won the latest and greatest phone and that I needed to click the link in order to win. I rolled my eyes and deleted it. I assume the old owner of this number had somehow gotten on a spammer's contact list because no one else had this number but Emma. If she'd taken Falcone's money, chances were she wasn't anywhere near Bar 53 when the shooting went down.

Without a second thought, I called Emma and was greeted by a familiar sound: ringing that led to nowhere. This time, the ringing stopped.

I held my breath. Was she finally going to answer?

"Hello. You've reached the voice mailbox of Emma. This inbox is full."

"Shit," I mumbled and hung up the phone. It seemed as if I wasn't the only one who was trying to reach her. I'd left only one voicemail for her when it had been a couple of days since I'd heard from her. This meant that other people were trying to reach her too, and she wasn't deleting the messages.

A sinking feeling filled my stomach. I hadn't known Emma all that long since she came to Falcone's after I had worked there. But in that time, I'd never known her to go this long without returning a call or text. Especially not when it came from me.

Being with Ace would have been very helpful right now. I believed he would know what to do. Hell, at the very least, he would have enough money and probably connections to throw at the problem. There was always the chance that Ace wouldn't give a damn and wouldn't do anything to help make this go away... but what was the point of focusing on him? Oh, that's right. He was at the front of my mind because I was having sex dreams about the man.

Then again, there was something else that I could do. Going to the police was an option. I could avoid telling the meat of the story, which included all of Falcone's stuff. I quickly washed the dishes I dirtied and left the kitchen to grab what I needed to go to the police station.

As I was getting my wallet, my phone vibrated, and I quickly picked it up. Another text message? Two in one day was unheard of for me since I moved to Dalhurst.

Emma: *Can't talk right now. I'll reach out when I can.*

I blinked rapidly, not believing the message I'd just gotten. There was no way that the police would investigate now based on this text. I thought I would feel relief at finally getting a response from her, but fear crept in instead.

How did I know that it was really her? It wouldn't take much for someone to use her phone to send me a text. And I had no way of tracking where the phone was or who might have had it. Nothing she said had been distinctive enough for me to confirm her identity.

Me: *Why can't you call me now? I'm worried. Also, a shooting happened at Bar 53. Call me back ASAP!*

I stared at my phone, willing her to respond, but there were no more messages. She didn't bother to call me either. These were all just more red flags that had been raised with her.

What the hell had Emma gotten herself into?

8

HARLOW

I couldn't believe how fortunate I was. Here I was, driving to Lindow Cemetery to visit Mama Robinson. The ride was uneventful outside of the rain that was falling. It fit the somber tone of the day and my being able to go visit her gravesite was a blessing.

When I explained to Chloe what I wanted to do, she wholeheartedly agreed to let me borrow her car to go visit Mama Robinson's tombstone. Her kindness seemed to be unwavering and right now I needed that even if I thought it was only a matter of time before something bad happened. Only thing was that I had to go the day before her death anniversary because Chloe needed her car all day tomorrow. Since I was fortunate enough to go at all, I jumped at the chance and promised that I would fill the car up with gas before I handed her back the keys.

I glanced at the pink flowers in the passenger seat that I had bought on the way here. They were her favorite color. I hoped they would do their part to brighten up Mama Robinson's grave.

I parked the car and walked up the road to where I knew her grave was. Nothing much had changed since she'd been buried here. I tried to hold back any emotions as I thought about the day she was laid to rest. When I spotted her tombstone, I couldn't stop the tear that had been holding on near the corner of my eye from falling. Even with all the shit that had been thrown my way recently, I made it.

"Hi, Mama," I whispered, but my voice still cracked slightly. "It's me, Harlow."

I took a deep breath before I continued. "I don't know if you can hear me, but I just wanted to tell you how much I miss you and that I love you so much. I wish that you were still here to talk to me and to guide me through this crazy stuff we call life. But you're not. And not a day goes by that I don't think about you."

The tears were in a free fall now. Controlling any part of my emotions right now wasn't going to happen. "I've made some mistakes that I'm not proud of, but I remember how you would say that I was only human. I'm allowed to make mistakes and learn from them. That's what I'm trying to do, and I promise that I'm going to make you proud."

And then I sobbed uncontrollably. I would have thought time would have made things like this easier, but it hadn't. Time didn't heal all wounds.

"You told me that I was one of the strongest people you knew and I could say the same about you. But right now I'm not feeling so strong. I feel completely broken, my spirit is shattered and I'm not sure what to do right now besides hide. You wouldn't have wanted me to run away from adversity, but I felt as if I had no other choice. I'm afraid and I don't know what to do now."

I bent my head to stare at the ground, but instead, I closed my eyes and let my grief temporarily swallow me whole. I tried to imagine her warm hugs that provided comfort no matter the occasion, but that only made me cry harder.

Memories of the happy times that we spent together pushed out the bad ones and I was able to slowly calm down. Once I could control my crying, I stood up and patted her tombstone before turning away and I walked back to Chloe's car. When I was safely inside, I dug into my purse and pulled out some tissues that I'd put in there this morning just in case this was to happen. I looked in the mirror and wiped my tears before stuffing the tissue back into my purse.

I stared at the woman looking back at me, wondering how the hell I'd gotten here. Forcing my eyes to close helped, along with taking a couple of deep breaths.

It was okay to break down sometimes.

I gave her gravesite a small sad smile and one last look. After I reassured myself that I wouldn't fall apart again, I put the car into drive and drove away from the cemetery. Having a good crying session and visiting Mama Robinson helped reinvigorate me. Whether I liked it or not, I had to be ready to take on the world and now I felt as if I could.

Was I about to do this? I stared at my blonde hair, hair I hadn't dyed since high school. I shook my head at the memory of the blue highlights I'd tried to add to my hair myself and how it hadn't turned out well.

I still had the opportunity to tell Chloe that I didn't want to color my hair tonight. But I'd already taken so many risks recently. What was the harm in another? Especially since this one was the least risky of them all.

I took a swig of the beer that was resting on the windowsill near my bed to calm my nerves. It didn't work.

"Ready whenever you are."

I turned to find Chloe standing behind me with a big smile on her face.

I nodded. "Let's do this." I said the words before I could think about them, so I couldn't dwell on them any longer.

"Well, let's get to it."

The entire process didn't take as long as I expected. I knew I had laughed more times tonight than I had in days. Soon I found myself staring in the mirror at my new hair color.

"It looks pretty good." I ran my fingers through my newly brown strands as I gazed into the tiny mirror sitting above the equally tiny sink in the bathroom.

"It looks better than good, Sam!"

My eyes widened before I could stop myself. It took me a second to realize that it was me who she was referring to. I gave Chloe a small smile and went back to look at my hair in the mirror.

Chloe had done a great job of helping me, and I was pleased with the results. I smiled at her, snatched the cheap beer that she'd offered me, and took a long gulp. It was my second beer of the night, having gotten a refill when we were waiting for the dye to do its job.

"Thanks for everything," I said.

"Don't mention it." She took her last sip of her beer and said, "I need to run downstairs real quick and grab another. Do you want one?"

I shook my head. "No, thank you. I'll start cleaning up things in here and maybe we can watch the television in the living room?"

"Okay."

Chloe left the room, and I began cleaning the mess we'd made with my hair-dyeing adventure. Thankfully, I didn't think it would take too long and soon I'd be able to put my feet up on the couch and relax if no one else in the house had already commandeered the living room.

A few minutes later, I heard Chloe call me from downstairs. I walked into the doorway of the bathroom and said, "Yeah?"

"Someone sent you a letter."

That was odd. The only person who knew I lived here was Emma, but why would she send me a package when she wouldn't even return my phone calls?

"Are you sure it's for me?" The question felt ridiculous leaving my lips, but I was too shocked to catch it.

"Definitely. It says 'Sam' on it."

The envelope was addressed to 'Sam'? I didn't tell anyone about that name and had come up with it on the fly. "I'll be down in a minute."

"Okay, I'll leave it at the bottom of the stairs."

I finished cleaning up the bathroom and walked down the stairs. There sat a white envelope with the name "Sam" scribbled across it with a black marker. Someone had dropped it off at the house as opposed to it being delivered by a service.

The hairs on the back of my neck were standing at attention. How had he figured out the name that I'd only given to my housemates and where I lived? I glanced at Chloe in the kitchen and walked into the living room to peek out of the window. I moved the blinds and almost screamed. Ian was sitting in a car outside of the building. As if he knew I was looking at him, he looked directly at me and gave me a small wave.

Falcone had found me and sent the man who hated me the most to stalk me. I shook as I backed away from the window, choosing to ignore the trouble that was now on my doorstep. The plan I'd cooked up to stay safe was fucked, and I had nowhere to turn.

I ignored the package for the rest of the evening until I found myself staring at it as I prepared for bed. Part of me thought I should toss it in the trash, but I couldn't deny that I was curious about what its contents might be. With a huff, I walked over to the envelope and picked it up.

Before I could debate with myself any further, I ripped open the envelope and pulled out a piece of paper. I read what they wrote on the note and the blood running through my veins froze over.

You can run, but you can't hide. You're going to pay for every single thing you've done, "Sam."

9

ACE

"Do you have an update for me?" I asked as the driver I hired drove us down the New York City strect. I opted to go into my office today to be close in case Kingston's guys from Cross Sentinel could spot Harlow if she came to visit the gravesite. As if he knew I was thinking about him, Kingston's name appeared on the screen with what I assumed was an update.

"Yes, our guys stayed outside and watched Robinson's grave all day and there was no sign of Harlow today. But we suspect that she might have come yesterday."

Shit. If I'd alerted them about it sooner, maybe we could have spotted her. "What gave you that impression?" I asked as the driver pulled to a stop at my destination. I held up my index finger, indicating that I needed one minute to wrap up the call.

"Someone laid flowers near the tombstone. There was a little rain on them, so we suspect they must have been there at least since last night. We waited to see if anyone else would show up today and nada."

"Okay, thanks. If you find out anything else, call me immediately." I hung up and stepped out of the car and toward the front doors of Bar 53. If the police were still sniffing around, there weren't too many signs of it anymore. I couldn't care less, however, because I only had one priority in mind.

"Hello, sir. How may I help you?"

I regarded the woman in front of me, assessing how I should handle this situation. Based on how she was studying me, trying to undress me with her eyes, it was clear she wouldn't mind if I fucked her right here in front of everyone. Too bad for her, she wasn't the woman I wanted, and the shift in that thinking felt strange, but right.

I moved those thoughts to the back of my mind and focused on the task at hand. "I'm meeting with Falcone today."

Her eyes widened before she headed back to the podium and used a phone to call down to his office. She nodded her head twice and then she looked back and gestured for me to come over to her.

"I was just told that he doesn't have a meeting with anyone on his calendar right now, so I'm going to have to ask you to leave."

She was right. I didn't have a scheduled meeting with Falcone, but he was going to want to see me. "Tell him Ace Bolton is here."

She watched me suspiciously but did as I requested. I had no doubt in my mind that he would want to see me, although he might not appreciate me coming unannounced. And frankly, I couldn't give a shit.

I took a step back from the podium and crossed my arms,

almost daring her not to do what I requested. When she whispered into the speaker, I took a moment to look around Bar 53, trying to see if I could spot Ian. He wasn't in my line of sight and that made me suspicious. Yes, it was perfectly reasonable for him to not be working today, but my gut told me something else was up.

When the woman in front of me cleared her throat, I looked back at her. "Mr. Falcone will see you now. Just head over to those stairs and walk down. You'll find someone standing in front of a door once you reach the basement. That's his office."

I didn't need her directions, but they confirmed Ian wasn't on site. The gist I'd gotten from him and from what Harlow had mentioned was that he lived to serve Falcone and just about every time I'd come here, he'd brought me down to Falcone's office. Ian not being here was telling. Where was the asshole?

I walked to Falcone's office and nodded at the security guard standing in front of the office door. He knocked, waited for a response, and then opened the door, allowing me to enter before closing the door behind me.

I found Falcone sitting behind his desk, intentionally not looking up at me, although it was obvious he knew I was there.

"Listen, I've had something come up. We can continue this conversation at another time."

The person on the other end of the line must have said something else because Falcone didn't immediately end the call. When he finally hung up, he acknowledged me. "Wasn't expecting you here today."

His underlying meaning was that he didn't appreciate me

showing up unannounced. I didn't care. "Surprises are my specialty."

"What do you want? To talk about the partnership I proposed?"

I sat down in the chair in front of his desk. "Where is she?"

He tapped a finger on his desk before resting his head on his hand. "Where is who?"

"Don't play stupid."

Falcone leaned back in his desk chair and put his feet on his desk. "I didn't peg you as the type of man to... lose your purchases."

"You didn't answer my question." I refused to take the bait. The shiftiness in his gaze told me he knew more than he was letting on.

"I'm under no obligation to do so."

"You don't want me on your bad side, Falcone." For a split second, his poker face fell, and I saw fear. I couldn't deny that seeing the vulnerability in his eyes was a thrill.

"Where. Is. She?"

"I don't know."

"Why do I get the feeling that you're lying to me?"

Falcone shrugged. "Because you always assume the worst. Your grandfather is like that too, so I can understand why—"

"Don't bring him up." I should have remained cool, but the slight bite in my words was enough to make Falcone spot a small weakness and start circling like a shark sensing blood. Funny how quickly the tables had turned, and Falcone assumed that he was now in control.

"Sore subject? It wasn't when I told you about me and him doing business together before."

That was before he'd called me repeatedly. He'd vowed to leave me alone, to let me run his company in peace, but with him trying to contact me, it was easy to see that something else was at play.

"You're not changing the topic here. Where are the people that Harlow interacted with? Ian? Emma?"

"Ian has the day off."

"Really? I thought you worked all of your employees to the bone."

"That's false." It was clear he was lying. "He wanted to take a day off and is allowed."

Of course, people were allowed to take days off, but I doubted Falcone did anything by the book here. I shifted to the other person in question. "And Emma?"

"She practically vanished. Haven't seen her in a few days."

I'd already known that to be the case, but this was an interesting development. "And you don't have people looking for her? Doesn't she owe you money?"

"The bitch is probably dead, so I'm not going to extend any resources in searching for something that will end up being a dead end."

It didn't go unnoticed by me that he didn't confirm whether she owed him money, unofficially confirming the information that Cross Sentinel found. I still wasn't convinced that this wasn't all an act on Falcone's end. I'd never heard of him being willing to just let someone go or not confirm whether they were alive.

"Why do you think she's dead?"

"Because she's too dumb to survive in this world on her own, especially without Harlow."

He was underestimating her. Interesting. This further

fueled my desire to find Emma because when I did, I would find out where Harlow was.

"Now, if you'll excuse me, I have other matters to attend to. After all, you dropped in on me unannounced."

"If I find out that you're not telling me everything you know…"

"I never tell anyone everything I know. What would the advantage be?"

"Your life."

Falcone chuckled. "Is that a threat, Mr. Bolton?"

"No." I stood up and walked toward the door. I looked over my shoulder at the man sitting behind his desk, thinking that any of the shit he built would protect him from my wrath. "It's a promise and I will take all of this shit down with me."

I didn't wait for Falcone to respond before I left his office in much the same fashion that I had walked into it. I meant every word. If I found out that Falcone was involved in all of this, he was fucked, and I would make sure that he suffered.

He was already on my shit list, but I knew there was more that I didn't know. And right now, he was worth more to me alive than dead. But that could all change quickly.

I expected it would. This situation ebbed and flowed depending on the information that I received.

And I got a sneaky suspicion that Ian's reason for not being there tonight had something to do with both the disappearances of Emma and Harlow. A key to finding Harlow could be through Emma, so finding her had just become a top priority.

I didn't like going back over the steps I'd already taken, but maybe I'd missed something. I grabbed the phone that I used to call Emma and wrote a text message instead. Why hadn't I thought of this before?

Me: *Shorty told me to reach out to you about a shipment. I can be reached at this number.*

If Emma thought I might try to score something from her, she might be more willing to respond. It was worth a shot.

I stepped back into the car and my ride back home was silent. I was lost in my thoughts about what the path forward was beyond hoping that Emma would respond to my latest attempt to contact her. It wasn't until I was walking up to my front door that one of my burner phones chimed, signaling that I'd just received a text message.

Emma: *Who is this? What do you want?*

Me: *To discuss a business arrangement. Shorty recommended you after you'd done business together. I heard you had ways of getting some of the things that I want. Figured this would be mutually beneficial to both of us.*

Emma: *How much and when?*

This was easier than I thought it would be.

10

———

ACE

Anderson opened the door for me, and I walked into my house. The same dreary house that only seemed to grow more depressing the longer Harlow wasn't here. She was still missing and lead after lead had come up empty. But the text from Emma burned like a fire in my pocket. It was the small beacon of light that could eventually lead me to Harlow.

"Is there anything I can get you, sir?"

"Yes, a finger of whiskey and bring it to my office."

"Yes, sir."

I left Anderson in the foyer and walked to my office. I was pleased to find that he'd already started a fire in the fireplace, providing a warm glow in my otherwise cold office. Some things in this house needed to change and Harlow's views about renovating the house came to mind. Once again, she'd taken over another section of my life when I least expected it.

When I'd closed the door behind me, my eyes landed on my desk, and I stared at the manila envelope Parker had given me the day Harlow left me. I'd refused to open it, in part due to not wanting to deal with the shit it would unleash.

Parker gave me the envelope, intending to give me a choice about whether I wanted to open it. He could have easily told me what it contained, but he didn't, leaving it up to me. Now the time had come to unleash whatever the envelope contained.

When I heard my office door open, I glanced up and Anderson was standing there with my drink in hand. Having something to drink while I viewed these documents would be helpful.

After he handed me the glass, I said, "Thank you."

Anderson nodded. "Let me know if you need anything else."

"Actually, I do. Can you find the three best interior designers in New York State? There are many things that need to be improved in this house and it's about time we started that process."

"Very well."

I waited until Anderson left my office before opening the top desk drawer and found the letter opener. I slid the blade under the flap before pulling out the contents. In it was a slew of papers that would take me some time to go through. I groaned because this would eat into time that I could use to track down Harlow or anyone who might know where she was.

There wasn't much I could do at this point. My meeting with Emma wasn't for another day so I couldn't do anything unless I wanted to drive through every street within a fifty-mile radius of my home in hopes of finding Harlow. And that was if she'd decided to stay nearby. If it were me, I probably wouldn't be anywhere near here.

I took a sip of my drink and skimmed the first page. I placed my glass down on my desk harder than I intended after I realized it would be worth it to pay more attention to what the documents said.

It looked to be a list of personal and business transactions over several years. Some of it did not surprise me. Paper trails about how he amassed the Bolton Fortune. Having dealings with various organizations, including the Cross family and the Mafia. I kept scanning the document, wondering if Parker had found...

Damn. If Parker was anything, he was very thorough.

He had notes on my grandfather's dealings with Falcone. I wasn't shocked to find that they'd done some deals on the black market, investing in companies that the other created and more. There were a couple of miscellaneous entries that I highlighted. My grandfather had invested a lot of money into whatever it was that Falcone was doing, which made me even more curious. I continued reading down the list in hopes of finding something that would help me decode what those sizable sums of money went to.

My search continued and I stopped on several entries labeled 'KH.' They, too, were several large sums of money that came from my grandfather's personal account. There was only one 'KH' that I knew. It couldn't be...

How much did he know about the businesses and associates that Kiki Hastings kept? I wouldn't be surprised if he'd paid her money to keep me once Mom died, so that shouldn't be staggering. Had he known what she did to me and chose not to act?

When my phone rang and I saw who was calling this time, I wasn't surprised. He had perfect timing. I debated whether I was going to answer while I pushed the papers that Parker gave me to the side after deciding that I wasn't going to mention what I'd just found. Instead of sending the call to voicemail, I answered.

"It's about time you took my call, Ace."

I closed my eyes to give myself a second to breathe before I responded to his comment that sounded more like an accusation. "I had some things that needed to be taken care of and figured you would text me if it was absolutely dire."

"You know I don't text."

And that wasn't my problem. "Well, why did you call me? I assume it wasn't just to check up on how I was doing."

"Just checking up on how the family business is treating you."

"You still sit on the board of directors, to which I deliver a report. You know exactly how the business is going. I have some other business I need to attend to if this is the only reason you decided to bless me with this call."

"Ace—"

The tone in his voice struck a different chord, but I couldn't quite place it. All I ever knew from him was disregard for anything related to me unless it had something to do with the family business.

"What?"

"Watch yourself."

"Is that a threat?"

"No, of course not. I truly mean to watch yourself. Word travels even to a remote island far away. We'll talk later."

The next thing I knew, the call had ended, and my whiskey was all but forgotten.

THE NEXT EVENING, I sat in my black sedan outside of a house that seemed all too familiar. It reminded me of the one I grew up in, a far cry from the mansion I lived in now.

But I remembered being happy. Not just a shell, void of many emotions and floating through life as I tried to conquer one company after another. But the emptiness that I usually felt increased tenfold because of Harlow's disappearance.

Getting one step closer to hopefully finding Harlow was what was driving the adrenaline careening through my body. I was somewhat surprised at how easy it was to set up a meeting with her, but I assumed that the drive to have a business transaction outweighed any precautions one would normally take.

I watched the home that she told me to come to for any signs of movement, but so far, I'd seen none. Although it was the middle of the day, there weren't many signs of life other than me on this quiet street. It reminded me of the street I'd found Shorty on.

I opened my jacket and glanced down at my gun. Did I think I'd have to use it tonight? No. But I'd brought it with me just in case because I didn't know what I was getting myself into.

A text message appeared on my dashboard, and I skimmed the quick note from Kingston.

Kingston: *My men and I are on standby down the street.*
Me: *Ok.*

My reply took slightly longer to type than usual because of my glove-covered finger. I'd called in backup just in case because I didn't want to underestimate Emma. If she was willing to mess with Falcone even though she no longer owed him money and, at the very least, be involved with drug trafficking, I didn't know who, if anyone, she was working for nor what she would be capable of. With Harlow's safety in the balance, I didn't want to take any chances.

When the clock on my dashboard hit ten o'clock, I opened the car door because it was time for Emma and me to meet.

After I closed the door behind me, I buttoned my suit jacket so as not to give her any indication that I was carrying a weapon.

I walked across the street, my stride eating up the distance between my car and the home she wanted to meet at quickly. After studying the front door to see what type of security she had, I turned my body so that I wasn't facing the doorbell camera. I rang the doorbell and waited for the woman of the hour to appear. When I heard the doors unlock, I braced myself, preparing my body to spring into action if need be.

"Hello and please come in—" She stopped short of finishing her sentence as she studied me in the doorway. It was clear that she'd recognized me immediately. I could see her thinking of what she should do next to get out of this predicament, but I didn't give her a chance to act. With my hand firmly on the door, I pushed my way into her home and slammed the door shut behind me.

I didn't give her a chance to finish what she was saying because it didn't matter. In the grand scheme of things, she didn't matter. "Where is Harlow?"

"I have no idea."

"Well, at least you aren't attempting to act as if you don't know her, but your answer isn't good enough. Where is she?"

"Fuck. I knew I shouldn't have trusted Shorty."

Good. I'd had a feeling that Shorty hadn't warned her about what I'd done to him because why would she even think about trying to meet with me? Maybe he was still pissed she'd given him a bracelet instead of paying him with money. I hadn't expected Shorty to be beneficial in any other way, but it turned out that he had no problem flipping a switch on Emma. The saying that there was no honor among thieves would fit this situation. But I could give a shit less about Shorty.

I took a step toward her, and she took a step back in return. The pattern continued until I had her back against the wall, and I was crowding her space, determined to intimidate her into telling me where Harlow was. "Where is she?"

"I don't know."

I pulled out the gun that I'd brought with me. "If you value your life, since you clearly don't care about Harlow's, you'll tell me where Harlow is. I have no problem shooting you right here, right now."

She swallowed hard and I smirked.

"How dare you say that I don't care about Harlow? I helped her get away from you."

The quiver in her voice told me that the courage she was trying to show me was bullshit. If she thought her remark was going to sting me, she was wrong. I refused to give her the satisfaction of seeing a reaction from me. It was inter-esting to see this side of her, given the impression I got of her when she ran into Harlow's arms the day we went to meet with Falcone together.

"If you don't tell me where Harlow is, and I know you know, your value to me ceases to exist, and I'll end it all right here. And then whatever scam you're running ends. I know more about you than you think I do." I shoved the barrel of the gun under her chin, and I watched her tremble slightly.

Her eyes darted around the room before landing back on me. "Fine. I'll tell you where she is. And then I want you to leave me alone, before I call—"

"I don't give a shit who you call. Just tell me where Harlow is."

When she finally told me where Harlow was, I put my gun away and said, "Now, I want you to stay away from her. I know about the shit you've been involved in."

"Get. Out."

I nodded my head at her before leaving the home. I snatched my phone out of my pocket and called Kingston.

Before he could answer, I said, "I have the address for where Harlow is staying in Dalhurst. Sending it to you now. Meet me there."

11

HARLOW

"**A**re you sure you don't want to come along?"

I gave Chloe a small smile and shook my head. "Nah. You guys go out and have fun. I'm going to hang out around here for the evening."

Chloe invited me to go out to a bar with some of her friends, but I didn't want to go out. It would take way too much effort to pull myself together to look presentable.

"Only if you're sure. We'd love to have you join us."

"Thanks for the invite, but no."

"Okay, fine. We'll see you later."

I waved at Chloe as she left, leaving me alone because our other housemates were also busy doing who knew what.

I hadn't left the house since I saw Ian's car parked outside. To be fair, I didn't have anywhere to go at the moment, but I knew it was only a matter of time before I had to leave because there was no way that I was going to be blamed if Ian decided to harm anyone here. But where could I go?

I took another bite of the ham and cheese sandwich I

fixed and chewed it slowly as I wrapped up another project. The virtual assistant freelance jobs that I'd picked up were one-off jobs and provided very little money for me to up and leave. Thankfully, I hadn't used all of my savings, but I didn't want to risk that running low too.

Think, Harlow. Think.

No matter how much I pushed myself to come up with a plan, nothing was coming to mind. Fuck. I'd barely gotten out of some situations before, but I wasn't sure if I was going to be as lucky this time around. With a sigh, I closed my laptop and stood up. I wanted a drink but didn't think I had any beer in the fridge.

I took my plate to the kitchen, washed it and checked the fridge. After confirming I didn't have anything besides water to drink, I walked back into the living room to grab my laptop and head to my room. As I was walking toward the stairs, I pulled out my key while mindlessly thinking about what I wanted to do this evening.

But that was short lived.

I jumped when I heard the back door slam open. What the hell was that? From my short time here, I'd put together a general idea of when people were around and when they weren't, and this was usually a time where no one was in the house except me. There was no need to slam the back door.

Maybe one of my housemates had arrived? Were they pissed? I shifted my body to look over the banister and my eyes widened when I saw what had caused the door to open.

"Have you opened my little gift for you?"

I took a step back. Was I seeing things? Because there was no fucking way this was happening. Then again, I should have suspected this. I let my guard down and now I was in this predicament.

"Surprised to see me?"

"Ian, leave now because I called the police before I came downstairs. They'll be here any minute." It was a lie that only I knew, but I hoped it would buy me time.

He smirked and held up his hand. He was holding a small device. "There's no way you could have called anyone from that shitty phone that fast. Looks like it's just you and me for a few hours until your housemates get home. There are plenty of things that I can think of that will keep us occupied."

Instead of waiting for him to attack me, I ran up the stairs toward my room. I could beat him upstairs with enough time to lock my door and buy myself some precious seconds. *Shit.* I still needed to open my door first.

As my foot hit the top step, Ian caught me and body-slammed me into the wall face-first.

"Ow!" I cried out, struggling against his hold.

"This brings me back to the night when we almost fucked." His hot breath in my ear made me want to throw up.

"We didn't almost fuck. You tried to rape me. Get off of me!" And now I was worried this time he would succeed. I felt his hand creep up my body until he found my ass. He grabbed a fistful and I started screaming, hoping that someone would hear me. But no one did. Instead of contin-uing with his assault, he dragged me into my room. He ripped my button-down from my body and tossed me on the bed. I shouted again as I tried to get up.

Ian's smirk turned downright frightening as he slowly

made his way over to me. I started screaming again. "I can't wait to hear those screams turn into you screaming my name when I'm fucking you."

"Never!" I yelled. Everything slowed down. It was as if my soul left my body, and I couldn't control anything that was happening. I used my bed as leverage to throw my body at Ian, fighting him with all my might. I had no other choice. If he was going to hurt me, I wasn't going down without a fight. A tinge of despair slid into my mind when I realized there was no way I was going to be able to get around him to run out of the door.

When he made a move to grab my neck, I tried to roll away from him. I could feel my adrenaline pumping through my veins. "Get away from me!"

Ian covered my mouth with a gloved hand. I tried to use my teeth to bite him but failed. When he tried to use his other hand to grab my wrist, I threw a punch and it landed on his cheek. It only startled him for a second, but it was enough for him to move his hand so that I could scream again.

Anger shone in his eyes. He swung his hand and slapped me in the face. The sting from the hit made me see spots. Soon, he was back on the bed. I gasped when I saw a gun in his hand. I wasn't sure how I'd missed him grabbing it, but it must have been when I was recovering from the hard slap that landed across my face.

He used one hand to hold the barrel of the gun under my chin while his other hand was everywhere. Fighting him was the only way out of this, even if I felt as if I wasn't any match.

"I was going to make this as easy as possible before I killed you, but now you've pissed me off."

He covered my mouth again and fear slid down my spine. My eyes widened as I saw the wicked look in his eyes. The hand not holding the gun grabbed one of my breasts hard, making me wince in response. He then moved down to the button of my jeans, which he quickly got rid of and unzipped my pants.

I heard a commotion coming from downstairs, but my attention was on Ian and what his next move might be. Pounding on the stairs gave me hope. The sound didn't deter Ian from his goal.

"What the hell is going on here?"

Relief flooded through my veins at the sound of his voice. Ace's voice sounded like a roar, freezing both Ian and me in our tracks.

While his appearance shocked the both of us, our reactions were completely different. Ace and I weren't on good terms, but the look he was giving Ian told me he was ready to murder him. Ian's eyes jumped between the two of us and I assumed he was trying to decide if he could take both of us. When Ian shifted the gun, I saw the slight shift in Ace's gaze. In one motion, Ace yanked Ian off of me and the breath I'd been holding was released. I scrambled to get up and grabbed one of the few things that I had in the room that was within arm's reach: the photo frame with the picture of Mama Robinson and me outside of The Attic.

I thought throwing the picture at his head might have knocked him out, but it didn't. The gun flew out of his hand and Ace tackled him, dragging them both into the narrow hallway outside of my room. I stood there stunned for a moment before I dove for the gun.

I tried to aim the gun at Ian, but between Ace and him fighting on the floor, I couldn't aim it at him. If it came down to having to shoot Ian, I wouldn't be able to make the shot without risking shooting Ace.

A scream left my throat when I heard yells from the front door and heavy footsteps ascending the stairs. Could it be the police? If it wasn't, how someone hadn't called the police due to all the banging and shouting in here was beyond me.

"Ace, get off of him."

The man knew Ace's name? Did they come here together?

"Not until I kill this fucker." Ace threw another punch and hit Ian in the cheek so hard that I took a step back.

"That can come later, but we need to move out of here now. Your girl here is scared."

I wasn't Ace's anything, but he was right about me being scared. Hell, terrified sounded more appropriate. Ace stopped hitting Ian and stood up, glaring at the man groaning on the floor. Ace nodded at the man who convinced him to stop hitting Ian and walked toward me.

"Are you okay?"

All I could do was stare at him. I couldn't find the words to say due to the rush of emotions flowing through me. Wondering what all had happened and how he too had known where to find me.

"I should have checked on you first," Ace said as he felt along my arms, examining for any injuries.

"You were trying to disarm Ian. I get it and I'm fine."

Ace studied me and cursed. "No, you're not." He quickly took off the black leather jacket he had on and placed it over my shoulders. When I looked down at myself, I saw what made him act this way. I'd forgotten that I was shirtless because Ian had snatched my top, exposing my bra and my stomach.

Shit. Had adrenaline caused me to forget?

Ace moved to block me from view with his body. He then took the gun from me and handed it to the stranger over his shoulder. "Here, Kingston."

Kingston took the gun and then Ace's attention was fully on me again. "Change your clothes. Pack the things you'll need immediately and whatever else will be brought to my home within twenty-four hours."

When I opened my mouth to say something, Ace's words stopped me. "This is not the time to argue because you are coming with me. Whatever you want to discuss can happen in the car."

My body moved before my mind did, and I started packing the things that I would need immediately. While I quickly threw items into as many bags as possible, I came across the bag that I'd thrown into the closet when I first arrived here.

"Ace?" I looked over my shoulder. His eyes met mine, but he said nothing, waiting for me to continue.

"I-I don't want what's in this bag."

Ace walked over to me and looked inside the bag. His eyebrows shot up before his stare centered on me. "Where did you get all of this money from?"

"Long story."

"And that's something else you can explain to me when we are in the car. Let's go."

I nodded, moved out of my closet, and found the smashed frame with Mama Robinson's photo in it. After taking a deep breath, I bent down to get a closer look at the frame. I shifted the broken glass out of the way and picked up the photo. I ran a finger over Mama Robinson's image before I walked over to my purse and placed the photo inside of it, along with the note from Ian. With my purse strap on my shoulder, I walked out of what was now my old bedroom with my head held high, hopeful that I would never have to see this place again.

12

ACE

After the loud commotion in Dalhurst, silence was the theme since I pulled away from the curb. Harlow said nothing as I drove behind Kingston's SUV and to be honest, I preferred it that way. The tension in the car was thick and I preferred to ignore it. I'd rather be alone with my thoughts as we traveled to a destination unknown because all that mattered right now was getting my hands on Ian and making him suffer.

Ian had a lot of fucking nerve. Hell, so had Falcone for that matter if he'd sent Ian to terrorize Harlow. I assumed they both suspected that no one would be there to stop their shit. And if Emma had been involved as I suspected she might have, there was a special place in hell reserved for her too.

The image of Ian touching her made me want to drag him out of the trunk of Kingston's SUV and torture him on the side of this road. But maintaining a cool head was the only way to prevail in this situation. At least for right now because

I knew the tides would change once I set my sights on him again.

"How did you know where to find me?"

Hearing Harlow's voice jerked me out of the thoughts swirling in my mind. I waited a beat before I responded, trying to give myself time to calm myself after spending the entire car ride thinking of ways to torture Ian. This was a mess that I created. It was because of me she left. It was because of me she didn't have the protection she needed. And my own faults were something I was working on coming to terms with. But for right now, I needed to focus on taking care of Harlow and making sure that Ian never did this to another person again.

I knew I should be honest, even if the truth felt like the worst thing in the world to tell her right now. "Emma, or whatever her real name is, told me."

"She what!" Harlow exclaimed, her mood doing a complete one-eighty from what it had been just a second before. "Why should I trust anything you say?"

"You think I would lie to you now even after I just saved you from Ian?"

"Stranger things have happened."

I would be the first to admit that her words stung me more than the punch Ian managed to land in our fight. However, I couldn't blame her for feeling this way.

This is a mess that you created.

Now, I was on track to fix my mistakes.

I knew deep down I should have taken a gentler approach since I was saying this to protect Harlow, but the words left my mouth before I could stop them. "You'll never see her again."

"You can't tell me who to see and who not to see, Ace."

"When it comes to saving your life? Yes, the fuck I can."

"You can't believe that Emma had anything to do with this."

"I can and I do. I don't know exactly how she was involved, but I don't doubt that she fits into this fucked-up puzzle some type of way."

When Harlow said nothing in defense of her friend, I glanced over at her and found a pained expression on her face. "What's wrong?"

"You know that money that I showed you back there?"

"Yes." I'd handed the money off to Kingston and his team because that was the last thing I wanted to deal with right now. My priority was to make sure that Harlow was safe and then murder the asshole that was currently being shoved around in the back of one of the Cross Sentinel SUVs.

"Emma gave it to me. The day I... left your place. She said she stole it from Falcone because he owed her. The reason why she gave some of it to me was so that I would have some type of money cushion while I tried to figure out what I was doing."

I tapped my fingers on the steering wheel as I thought about what Harlow had just admitted to me. Did Emma get that money from Falcone, or was it from somewhere else? I knew she was in the drug business to a certain extent, so that wouldn't be a surprise. Could all of this have been a setup so that Falcone and Ian knew where Harlow was?

Those questions all needed to be answered, but for now, I needed to focus on keeping Harlow as calm as can be. "Now that I know Emma has her hands dirty in Falcone's money that is even more reason to stay away from her."

What was interesting about this was that it seemed Emma *owed* Falcone money now. And if I could track her down easily, he could try to do the same. Whether he would succeed was another matter.

"Fine. It's not like I can get in touch with her, anyway."

"Why couldn't you contact her?"

Harlow sighed. "She told me she couldn't talk to me right then but would reach out when she could. That was days ago and was the last time I heard from her."

But she had no problem being reached when she thought she had a prospective drug deal going down. There was clearly more here that I didn't know and the more questions I asked, the deeper this shit ran. But for right now, we had a more pressing matter at hand.

"Where are we going?"

Harlow's question brought me out of my thoughts. "Somewhere so that I can handle Ian."

"Handle him how?"

I looked at her but didn't say a word. When our eyes connected, I watched as hers widened considerably. I didn't need to explain myself further.

"Ace, why would you—"

"Don't finish that sentence. We're not going to debate what I am and what I'm not going to do."

The rest of our drive was in complete silence. When Kingston's SUV pulled up in front of a warehouse, I parked behind him and together, Harlow and I watched as he and three of his men walked to the trunk of the SUV and pulled a hooded Ian out of it. The three men walked him into the abandoned building while Kingston walked over to me. I rolled down the driver's side window for Kingston.

"I'll watch Harlow while you go in there and handle Ian."

"Okay, give us a second."

He nodded his head, and I closed the window.

"You're not leaving me here with him."

"Harlow, this is the safest place for you to be."

"I'm not going to sit in this car while you do whatever you're going to do to Ian when I'm the one he tried to rape... Not you."

There was so much more in the underbelly of her comment that I didn't have time to get into. "You still don't get it."

"Don't get what?"

This wasn't where I wanted to have this conversation, but she didn't leave me much of a choice. "While Ian didn't physically hurt me, he hurt you. He touched what was mine and that motherfucker is going to pay."

"I'm not yours. You didn't want me, remember?" Harlow's words came out in a whisper, but I heard her as clear as day. She didn't turn to look at me as she was saying the words, instead choosing to look straight ahead so I couldn't get an accurate read of her face. What she said would take too much to dive into right now, and I had business that needed to be tended to right now. The rest of this could be figured out later.

"Stay here with Kingston."

"No. I'm coming with you. I want to see what happens."

"It's safer for you out here."

"I don't want to be safe. I want to watch him suffer."

There was no way I could deny her that.

13

HARLOW

Even after everything that had happened tonight, I still couldn't believe the scene unfolding in front of me. The warehouse that we'd entered could best be described as a torture chamber, with Ian hanging by his limbs while Ace beat him with punches and kicks. Ace looked over at me, and his heavy breathing sounded like it was all around me. As if he heard my thoughts, Ace looked at me before turning to one of the guys that were watching him beat up Ian.

"Let him down."

I watched as the men I now learned who were a part of Cross Sentinel let Ian drop to the floor. Kingston had given the order that whatever Ace said, goes. When he groaned, I couldn't tell if it was from pain or relief, not that it mattered, anyway.

Ace walked over toward me, concern shining in his eyes. "Are you okay?"

I nodded and crossed my arms in an attempt to protect myself from the scene that had unfolded in front of me.

"Do you want in on this?"

"What do you mean?"

Instead of responding, Ace pulled back his jacket and pulled out a gun. I never imagined I would be in this position. But I couldn't deny that the temptation to take the gun out of his hand was there.

"Do you know how to shoot a gun?"

"I went to a shooting range twice, so I have a general idea."

"If this is something you want to do, take the gun. If not, that's fine too, but no matter what, Ian is going to die within the next few minutes."

I stared at the gun before taking it out of his hand. Ace shifted his body and together we walked back toward Ian. I held the gun up and wrapped my hands around the grip.

"Pull the trigger, Harlow."

My hand shook slightly as my eyes jumped from Ace to Ian's royally fucked-up face. It hadn't taken Ace much time to find Ian, and when he did he didn't hold back. We all had ended up in an abandoned warehouse that Ace said belonged to a friend. I didn't ask questions.

Ace had done a number on him, and I wasn't sure Ian had landed a hit based on what I could see of Ace.

"She can't fucking do it. Killing people is more your style than hers."

I licked my lips and felt my entire world shake as I tried to calm my nerves. He was right. I couldn't do this. I couldn't take someone's life.

Ace focused his eyes on me, drawing me in with his stare. "This piece of shit tried to rape you and kill you. You can kill him."

"It's not my job to judge him."

Ian snorted. "She wouldn't even be able to kill me if she knew what happened to Cynthia Robinson."

The blood in my body ran cold. "What the hell do you know about Mama Robinson?"

"I know she's the reason why you came to Falcone for money. By the way, he's not going to be too thrilled about the 'show' you've put on here."

Anger grew from deep within me. His manipulation was clear, but I still tried to maintain a level head. "Tell me what you know about Mama Robinson."

"I don't have to tell you anything."

That was it. The anger boiled over. I turned to my right and fired a shot, slightly shaken that I hadn't been able to control myself. "Tell me what you know about my mother's death."

It was the first time in a long time that I'd acknowledged that she was my mother. The pain that I felt because she wasn't here rose to the surface.

I glanced at Ace, and he dipped his head. I hadn't been seeking his approval for my actions but having him on the same page warmed me. Ian's eyes jumped from where I shot and back to me, his mouth wide open. Surprise, mother-fucker. "If you don't start talking—"

"Okay, okay." Ian's words rushed out as if he'd just completed a marathon. "Falcone made it so that you had to come to him for the money to pay for your adoptive mother's funeral."

"What do you mean, made it so that I had to?"

He sighed wearily as I watched as some of the cockiness

he loved to display fell from his face. "Cynthia Robinson also came to Falcone for money."

I stared at Ian. "You're a liar."

"If it's a lie, Falcone told it."

I glanced at Ace. "Did you know about this?"

"My research told me that Cynthia received a large sum of money, but I couldn't track from where or from who."

"We'll need to talk about how much of my history you've dug into later." My eyes landed back on Ian. "But you're also full of shit, so how do I know it's true?"

Ian coughed, I assumed to relieve some of the pain he'd had to be feeling from Ace's beatdown. "Falcone told me a story about it. NYU wasn't cheap and you needed some money to fund part of your last semester. She made sure that you finished by any means necessary. Between what she had in savings and Falcone's loan, she paid the fees. That was how he made it so easy for you to reach out to him about paying off Robinson's debt."

How would he know that if Mama Robinson hadn't gone through Falcone to secure the loan for my schooling? I remember getting a notice about money being due and needing to be paid in order for me to get my degree. I tried to take some deep breaths to calm myself down, but they weren't working.

Sorrow swam through my veins as I realized that the reason all of this had happened was because of me. Mama Robinson was doing her best to provide the finest educational opportunities. And the guilt that I felt wouldn't be leaving me anytime soon.

"Although she wasn't biologically your mother"—his

smirk gave me a hint of what he was about to say—"you were both stupid enough to borrow from the same man."

And just like that, nothingness filled my bones. Thoughts about sparing Ian's life fled my mind. I couldn't bring Mama Robinson back, but there was one thing I could correct.

"Thanks for the story, but you're still the scum of the earth. I hope this bullet sends you to hell where you belong."

Fear flashed in his eyes, and I refused to deny the thrill that it gave me. "Wait, Harlow, I told you what you wanted."

I listened to him for the last time. I didn't pull the trigger. Ian thought I'd saved him. But I had another idea in mind.

The anger I felt from everything he'd done to me was paramount. "Can we cut his dick off?"

Ace looked at me, and his eyes narrowed. "Are you sure about—"

"Yes." I turned my attention back to the wide-eyed man who'd lost any hint of attitude and snark. "He tried to rape me and just shooting him won't be enough to make him suffer. Cut his dick off."

Ace stared at me, probably wondering if I would call the whole thing off. When I didn't, he nodded to the same man who let Ian down. The guy was joined by two other men and once Ian was pinned down, I watched as they removed his cock. His yells were music to my ears.

After letting him carry on for several minutes, I was over this whole night. It was time to put an end to all of this. I aimed the gun the best I could and announced, "I'm shooting him."

A loud bang filled the room, followed by silence. My hand shook slightly as I measured what I'd done.

"You didn't care to seek revenge for yourself. You only

were able to pull the trigger when it came down to him talking about someone you loved."

Ace's words couldn't draw me from the display in front of me. The blood and other matter that was seeping out of Ian was enough to haunt me for years. But I felt no remorse. He deserved to be six feet under and then some.

It took me a moment to gather my thoughts and respond to Ace. "It's because I'd already gotten over the damage he'd caused me. But him throwing around Mama Robinson's name... didn't sit right with me. Why did you wait for me to shoot at Ian before you followed suit? You could have easily taken him out based on the bullet lodged in his head. You're an excellent shot."

"How do you know you weren't the one who shot him in the head? I heard a second gunshot after mine."

He chuckled when I gave him a look that said he was full of shit.

"It was something that you needed to do. He'd tormented you, tried to rape and kill you. Although it took everything in me not to shoot him right after I'd fucked his face up, I held out for you. It just made sense."

"You know what else makes sense?" I asked, as I finally looked at Ace. I found him staring back at me and there was something different about his eyes as they studied me.

"What's that?"

"Having Falcone's head on a silver platter."

"I think we can arrange that."

14

HARLOW

I was still in shock about what I'd done. I'd ordered a man's dick cut off and helped kill him this evening. Should I feel remorse? Happiness? I couldn't process my feelings.

On the one hand, I didn't feel guilty about Ian no longer walking this earth. He'd caused enough trauma to last a lifetime. But who made me the person that should judge who got to live and die? Mama Robinson's death had taken a huge toll on me and was there someone out there wondering where Ian was? Wondering when he was coming home? Never.

"What was that?"

Ace's voice cut through my thoughts. I hadn't realized I spoke out loud.

"Nothing. I was just thinking."

Ace seemed to accept that answer and we fell back into a silence that was as comfortable as one could be after murdering someone.

"So, you dyed your hair."

I looked down at my brown strands. "I did. Felt the need for a change."

"I like it."

I scoffed. "I don't remember asking you if you did."

"If I want to share my opinion, I'm allowed to. After all, I saved your life."

"And no one asked you to."

The adrenaline from the evening was wearing off and, in its place, came anger. Was I grateful that Ace had shown up when he did? Yes, because I wasn't sure I would have had the same good fortune against Ian that I had the first time he attacked me.

"Watch your tone, Harlow."

His scolding was enough to stop me from egging him on while continuing to feed the anger I felt. Arguing with him right now wouldn't help with anything and I attributed part of my rage to what I'd just gone through. I took several deep breaths to calm myself down.

"Ace, can you turn some music on?"

He did so without inquiring further and I laid my head back and closed my eyes. I didn't blame either of us for not saying much, but I needed something to fill the dead space. Anything that could help distract me from the thoughts flying through my head.

I didn't know how long I stayed like that, but when I felt the car slow down and park, my eyes popped open. I looked out the window and then back at Ace.

"What's this?"

"A hotel," Ace replied matter-of-factly.

"Obviously because it's the Olympus Hotel. And I

remember you taking me here before, but what are we doing here?"

"I didn't want to drive back to my home, so we're staying here for the night."

It brought back memories of the passionate night we spent here after going to Elevate. It seemed like such a long time ago now, although it had only been a few weeks.

"At this rate, you might as well buy a condo in the city or something." My response came out more sarcastic than intended, and I bit the corner of my lip. I attributed my sassiness to attempting to process what had happened today.

"It's something I've debated doing."

"Of course you have."

He didn't respond because the valet appeared next to his door, and we soon found our way upstairs to the penthouse suite of the hotel. He let me in the room first before closing the door behind us.

"Is it okay if I take a shower?" The question fell from my lips before I could stop it. It felt weird to be asking for permission, but this place felt foreign to me, even though I've stayed in this penthouse suite before.

You don't belong here.

He grabbed my hand and spun me around to face him. "Whatever thought ran through your mind just now, erase it. You don't have to ask for permission to bathe."

Ace took his time studying me, and I wondered if he'd forgotten all about my request. He used the back of his hand to caress my cheek and I leaned into him, hoping that it would lead to more. I was still angry about what had happened between us, but his touch did something to me that I couldn't explain.

His fingers found their way into my hair, and he pulled on it, forcing my head up. It was enough to shock me, but not enough to hurt me. My lips parted slightly as I wondered what he was about to do next. It was then that I noticed the slight shift in his eyes before his face descended toward mine.

When he leaned down and claimed my lips, I gasped, and he slipped his tongue between my lips. I couldn't believe this was happening.

The desperation he felt for me was clear and how much I missed him came pouring out of me and into our kiss. I wanted him as much as he wanted me. I needed him as much as he needed me.

But he'd told me he didn't want me. Yet, he came after me, directly contradicting his actions when he told me he wanted to break our arrangement off.

I broke away first and immediately regretted it. Part of me wanted to keep kissing him and exploring this new feeling, but there was still so much we needed to figure out about ourselves and each other.

"I guess I should take that shower."

"And you don't want any company, sweetness?" He'd held his eyes closed for a second too long. His breathing was harsh, like what I'd heard in the warehouse before Ian met his demise.

I shook my head even though hearing him use his nickname for me warmed me considerably. "Not this time, Ace."

"I'll be in the living room for the time being if you need anything."

I watched him turn away and just before he reached the door, he looked over his shoulder.

"You don't know how much turmoil you put me through

when you left."

I was taken aback by his comment, but it didn't stop me from responding. "I wouldn't have left if you hadn't pushed me away."

Ace nodded. "I know that now."

After he left the room, I couldn't take my eyes off of the space he'd left. Instead of dwelling on it, I walked into the bathroom and found everything I could ever need. Of course, Ace had made sure that my every need was met. But that couldn't stop my mind from racing as I thought about the events from tonight. What normally would have been a relaxing moment was making me anxious. When I noticed my hand shaking slightly and I couldn't control it, I turned the water off and dried myself off. When I stepped into the bedroom, I found silk matching pajamas laid out on the bed. Ace really had thought of everything.

I changed into the clothes and left the bedroom. What I hadn't been expecting to find was Ace staring out the window, looking out onto the city's skyline. Sometimes I forgot how beautiful this city could be. But I couldn't take my eyes off of the man standing in front of the window.

The glow of the city's skyline outlined his broad shoulders, casting a mysterious glow around him. While I felt that I knew Ace to a certain degree, there were still parts of him he kept hidden from me. I wished he would entrust me with the things that he kept close to the chest, but then again, I didn't completely trust him. After all, he didn't want to be involved with me anymore, even though our relationship had evolved past our initial meeting.

"Come here."

His voice was barely above a whisper. But I heard him

loud and clear, and his voice made me suck in a quick breath. When I walked up to him, he tucked me into his side, pulling me closer to him. Being in his arms again made me feel safe, yet conflicted. Deep down, I told myself that I shouldn't get used to this because he'd have no problem throwing me out on my ass when he was tired of me.

And all of this left me with a lot to think about.

I AWOKE FROM A RESTLESS SLEEP, slightly disoriented. A few deep breaths helped me clear the fog in my brain and piece together where I was. The storm raging outside of this bedroom window greeted me, convincing me that it was a prelude to how the rest of the day was going to go. With a heavy sigh, I pulled the blankets off me and stood up. I heard nothing that led me to believe that Ace was awake too, but given how big this suite was, that didn't mean much.

Being this close, yet so far from him did nothing but muddle my thoughts and feelings. I longed to sleep next to him again, but the rejection that I felt reigned supreme.

My dwelling on all of it wasn't going to get me the answers that I wanted but finding and talking to Ace would. I debated walking out of the room in my pajamas but figured looking more presentable would make me feel less self-conscious and buy me time before I had to face him.

When I'd replaced the pajamas with a T-shirt and jeans and had thrown my hair up in a ponytail, I walked out of the bedroom and into the living room.

I found Ace in the living space. I wasn't shocked to find him in a white button-down and black slacks. What shocked me was him not having his computer or phone in sight. Instead, he was watching television.

When he saw me out of the corner of his eye, he looked at me and stood. He walked toward me with a small smile on his face. "Did you sleep well?"

"As well as could be expected."

"That's all we can ask for right now. I ordered brunch and it should be here within the next few minutes."

Once again, Ace had thought of everything. I wasn't ungrateful and of course, he was prepared for today as if he hadn't been involved in a murder last night. Whereas my mind was a jumbled mess, his seemed to operate on cruise control. He was cool, calm, and collected until the very end. Because of that, I was envious of him.

"Ace, we need to talk about... well everything."

"I know and we both need to eat. We can knock two things off the to-do list at the same time."

He had a good point. After standing in his arms last night, gazing out at the New York City's skyline for who knows how long, I'd gone to bed. Ace offered to take the other bed in the suite, and I didn't stop him. While I twisted and turned endlessly throughout the night, I debated with myself whether it was worth throwing out all of my logic and crawling into his bed, but I didn't. Although I missed the feel of his arms around mine and the touch of his lips, there was too much at stake, including my dignity.

The knock on the door signaled the food had arrived. Ace took care of letting the server in and allowing him to set up our food. Once all of that was done, Ace and I sat across from each other in a silence that I couldn't decide was comfortable or not.

I took a sip from the orange juice that had been poured for me and cleared my throat. When I looked up, I found Ace's dark-brown eyes staring back at me. His facial expression was unreadable.

"How many people have you killed?"

Ace's head tilted slightly. "That wasn't what I was expecting you to ask first."

"I'm happy that I can be the one who surprises you once in a while instead of the other way around."

Ace raised an eyebrow. "You're full of surprises. Trust me."

"And you're avoiding answering my question."

"Touché, but there is something I want to know first. Why did you ask me that?"

I licked my lips and said, "Because you felt too comfortable taking Ian's life. It took some convincing and for him to mention Mama Robinson for me to do so. You had no problem beating him to a pulp and then shooting him."

Ace rubbed a hand across his mouth. "And you're sure you want to know the answer to this question?"

I could tell that he was stalling, but it was a valid question. Would knowing the answer to this question change how I viewed him?

"Yes, I need to know."

"Maybe around thirty-five to forty? That's on the low end."

My fork fell out of my hand and landed on my plate. "You don't even know the exact number?"

Ace shrugged but said nothing.

"That doesn't bother you?"

"That I murdered people or don't know how many people I've killed?"

"Both."

"Nope, because they deserved to die. Are you feeling guilty about Ian?"

I thought about my answer for a moment while I ate a piece of my bacon. "Sort of. I still think he deserved what he got, but there is a hint of remorse." I took a deep breath before I continued, "There's something else I need to admit."

"What is that?"

"Remember when you asked me about the mark on my neck and I told you I got it in a car accident?"

Ace nodded slowly, but his stare was what made me nervous about telling him.

"That was from Ian. This wasn't the first time he tried to… rape me, but I got away. It was the catalyst for my participation in the auction."

Ace was quiet at first and I felt my comment hanging in the air. Then I saw the fire in his eyes. Ian's death might have been his greatest blessing. "I don't have an ounce of guilt about that fucker being six feet under right now. I wish I had known that he'd touched you the first time and I would have dealt with him before it came to this."

"At the time, there's no way I would have told you about Ian."

"And why is that?"

I sighed and looked down at my plate. "Because I didn't trust you."

"And do you trust me now?"

It felt as if his words had a hold on me and forced my eyes to look at him. That question was a loaded one.

"Harlow?"

"I guess I'm forced to on a certain level. Especially after last night."

Ace's expression darkened. "So, it's not because you want to."

I pushed my plate away from me because I'd lost my appetite. I sat up straighter, refusing to be intimidated by the weighted look in his eyes. "You rejected me when I thought that whatever we had going on had evolved into something more. Do I blame you entirely for that? No, because I should have been better prepared."

If I could have given myself a high five, I would have. My voice didn't waver, and I maintained eye contact the entire time I spoke. Although I missed his touch, being away from him had a positive effect on me, and I was proud.

"Do you know why I wanted to quit the arrangement we had?"

I shook my head and waited for him to explain.

"Because I didn't want to hurt you. I still have things I'm trying to work through, and it felt as if you were getting too close."

His honesty moved me because I hadn't been expecting him to say anything close to what he'd just admitted.

"Then there's the fact that I almost hurt you the night after we went to Elevate—"

"Ace, I'm not concerned about that, okay?"

He shook his head. "Well, I am. You deserved better than that and it was one reason I wanted to give you an out from the arrangement."

"What was the other?" I whispered the question and was surprised that he heard me.

He reached over and grabbed my hand, softly caressing

my fingers before he spoke. "Part of me wanted to push you away because you should have all the happiness in the world and I knew I couldn't give that to you, especially under the guise that I bid and won you at an auction."

It wasn't just his confession that sucker punched me in the gut. It was the softness of his voice that I wasn't used to hearing as well. I swallowed hard and tried to calm my racing heart as his words hung in the air.

"Was that too much for you?"

The normal gruffness and confidence that usually laced his words were back.

"No, but it's given me a lot to think about."

"Good. Do you have anything else you want to discuss?"

I debated saying yes because I wanted to keep this going, but I knew that we'd experienced a breakthrough that I didn't want to ruin if we continued down this path and hit a point where we'd gone too far. Also, I wanted some time to myself to think more about what he'd said.

"No, I think this conversation went well."

With that, I left the room. It was then that I realized that I'd forgotten to ask why he'd finally kissed me.

15

HARLOW

A week later, I found myself sitting in a car on the way to who knew where. It was the first time I'd been out of the penthouse suite since we'd arrived. Ace had mostly kept his distance from me, and I assumed it had more to do with the kiss than anything else. I didn't have the motivation to ask him.

Ace had offered to have any book I wanted to be delivered to the suite and I took him up on it as a way to keep me busy. Being able to keep mostly to myself was a good thing, but it made me long to be with Ace. The conflicting emotions that I had about him weren't resolved in the time we saw each other several times a day or when we were apart. I wanted to talk to him but understood that keeping a distance between us was helping me figure some things out.

"You definitely weren't kidding when you said that you were looking at places in the city, huh?"

"I rarely joke around, Harlow."

He had a good point. Ace didn't try to be funny, although some of the things he would say could be considered funny.

I covered my mouth as a yawn escaped. "Are we finished with the grand tour of New York City?"

"Nope. One more place we have a showing for and then we can head back to my place."

The drive to our destination was short and I couldn't be more grateful. After visiting seven potential locations, I was tired. I didn't think this was what Ace had in mind when he said he had some things to do before we left the city, but here we were.

We were greeted in the lobby by Bennett, the property manager of the building, and whisked upstairs on an elevator that would take us to the apartment that Ace had his eyes on. I looked down at my clothes and how the two men next to me in this elevator were dressed. I couldn't help but feel completely out of place. Why hadn't I taken the time to see if I had something more appropriate to wear to this? Oh, it was because I hadn't known that this was what we would be doing today.

While Ace and Bennett chatted among themselves, I tried to stop myself from berating myself for being somewhere I shouldn't be. I chalked my feelings up to being tired because I hadn't felt this way while we toured the other places we visited.

When the elevator chimed, announcing we had made it to the floor the apartment was on, Ace held the door as I stepped out followed by Bennett. We all walked down the hallway in silence and while we waited for Bennett to open the door, Ace grabbed my hand and gave it a small squeeze. I looked up at him and he lifted his eyebrow.

Before I could react, Bennett opened the door and spoke first. "I'm going to let you two look around first and then I'll come in for the official tour and answer any questions you may have."

"Thank you," Ace said before allowing me to walk in first. Bennett closed the door behind us, and Ace and I were once again alone.

"What happened?"

"What do you mean 'what happened?'"

"Why did you become quiet all of a sudden?"

I glanced down at my shoe before looking back up at Ace. "I'm just getting tired." That wasn't exactly a lie, but it wasn't the whole truth, either.

"Harlow, I can tell when you're avoiding answering my questions."

I rolled my eyes because I couldn't help myself. Of course, he called me out. "I feel like I don't belong here. I couldn't afford to live in a place like this in a million years. Hell, just look at what I'm wearing. I stick out here and it just became apparent to me."

"No one is judging you or thinks that you don't belong. You are supposed to be in whatever room you're in and never think otherwise."

A tear fell from my eye, and I quickly wiped it away. Admitting how I felt to Ace had taken courage because it was normally something I would have kept tucked away from the world in order to protect myself. Here I was freely admitting it to the man that I had let hurt me emotionally.

"I want your opinion on this place. What do you think?"

At each of the previous locations, he'd asked me what I thought, and I'd been honest about what I liked and didn't like about each. Instead of answering him right away, I stepped away from him, giving myself the opportunity to look around. I went from room to room, exploring the layout and how it all came together to make the apartment.

Stunning is what could best be used to describe the space. It was an open concept and the flow from the living room to the kitchen worked seamlessly. There were three bedrooms and four bathrooms. While the penthouse was in Manhattan, out the window, you could see Brooklyn's skyline and the East River. I didn't know how expensive this place was, but if I had to guess, I would assume between three to four million dollars based on the location alone. It seemed out of this world that someone could afford something this expensive.

When I walked into the master bathroom, I sighed. I could really see myself taking long baths in the massive tub sitting in front of me. I shook my head, removing thoughts of me ever staying here. This wasn't my home, and it never would be.

A creak from the wooden floor made me turn and I saw Ace standing behind me. "What do you think?"

I walked toward him and gave him a small smile. "This place is stunning. By far the best one we've toured so far today."

"Is there anything you would change about it?"

I walked around him, and he placed a hand on the small of my back as we walked back into the living area. "Not much, outside of paint colors. I think something warmer would fit the walls versus the white paint that's there now."

As I finished talking, Bennett entered the room, greeting us with a smile. "Can I answer any questions you have about this apartment?"

Ace and I swung around to face Bennett, but it was Ace who answered. "We'll take this place."

Both Bennett and I looked at Ace wide eyed.

"Are you sure there isn't—"

Ace cut him off. "I know what I want, and we want this apartment. Let's start the paperwork."

Once the shock wore off, it wasn't lost on me that he had said *we* would take this place.

THE ISSUES I had with Ace were still bubbling under the surface as he drove us to his estate. The downpour of rain that started when we left the city did little to help dissuade my mood and also made the trip take longer.

Conversation that would usually make the journey go quicker failed us. The soft jazz music was supposed to be a buffer for our silence but served as a quiet countdown to the inevitable. It was a blessing and a curse because it gave me plenty of time to sit here with my thoughts and for my anxiety levels to increase. It was because we were going back to his home, the place that had become my prison. While the dynamics felt different, I was still going back to when I felt captive for a time with him.

Ace parked his car in front of his home, and he turned his head toward me. Before he could say anything, though, I hopped out of the car and into the pouring rain.

With the rain pelting down on me once I exited the car, it didn't take long for me to get soaked almost to the bone. I couldn't force myself to move when I knew I should. A decision needed to be made and quick.

I stood outside of his home as the rain pelted my body. The logical solution would be to walk up to the door and knock, but I couldn't. I was back where I started and felt horrible, but once again, I was left with no other choice. Now whether he would protect me was another matter entirely, but I had only two options in this scenario: get back into Ace's good graces or die. If I ran, I'd be looking over my shoulder for the rest of my life, and it would only be a matter of time before Falcone found me.

I swiped at my hair that lay across my face and it wasn't until Ace came around and tossed a jacket over my head that I ran with him toward the front door.

The door opened and Marnie walked out, attempting to open her umbrella to guard herself from the rain. It took a second before she noticed us. When she did, her mouth dropped open.

"Get inside! Quickly, both of you!"

We rushed past Marnie and into the foyer, water dripping from our bodies. Marnie quickly ran into a bathroom on the main level and handed both Ace and me a towel to dry off.

"I'll go get Anderson to help here."

"No," Ace said, stopping Marnie before she could turn away. "Let Anderson enjoy his night off. The storm is bad, so if you want to stay the evening, that's fine too. Harlow and I can manage on our own."

Ace's phone rang. When he answered it, I saw his expression change from passive to angry. Instead of waiting for his next move, I turned to Marnie.

"Do you know if the guest room I was staying in still has the clothes Ace bought for me?"

"As far as I know, it does."

"Thank you." I gave her a small smile before I turned on my heel and hurried up the stairs. I wanted to get these wet clothes off me and if I could avoid Ace for the time being, I was more than willing.

It took a few minutes for me to pick out an outfit and braid my hair. Blow-drying my hair seemed like a bigger hassle than I wanted to deal with right now, so a braid would do. I walked back down the stairs and found that someone had started the fireplace in the living room. The warmth from the fire was soothing and helped calm some of my nerves about being here again.

I jumped when a door tore open, slamming against the wall behind it. I refused to look over because I had a feeling I knew what I would find: a furious Ace Bolton.

A week ago, fear had dominated my thoughts as Ian tried to finish the job he'd started weeks ago. But the mixture of emotions that I currently felt was more complicated to pinpoint. Fear was still there, but it wasn't that I was afraid of him. I was afraid of what he might do once he found out the truth about everything. He had become the constant in my life even when he'd driven me away when he said we couldn't be together anymore.

His measured footsteps sounded more like pounding on the floor as he walked closer to the living room. I was thankful that I'd chosen to sit here, meaning that my back was toward the door. I didn't want to see his face when he entered the room.

While my body might not be soaking wet from the rain, a shiver ran through me because the footsteps had stopped, and I could feel him staring at my back. Nerves had built as I'd gotten dressed and waited for him in the living room as I wondered what our first interaction in this house would be like. There were still so many things that were left unsaid and the longer he stood there not saying a word, the more shame crept into my mind. I'd made a vow not to return to this place because I refused to be somewhere I wasn't wanted, and now I was back where I started.

Memories of how I felt before I'd finally found my forever home with Mama Robinson were dancing at the edges of my mind, but I refused to let them in because I knew tears would follow. This was not the time to fall apart, especially in front of him. I reminded myself that the reason I was here was because he'd saved my life and he was the only one who could protect me from Falcone. I also didn't want anyone else to get hurt.

The wait for him to address me had become unbearable. I took a deep breath, looked over my right shoulder, and found the man of the hour standing there, his gaze trained on me, just as I had suspected. His expression was unreadable, making it difficult for me to know how to react.

Instead, I did the only thing I could think of. I whispered, "Hey."

The hoarseness of my voice was a mystery to me at first. I didn't feel sick to warrant the change, but the emotional toll this was taking on me was more than likely the root cause.

Ace didn't respond with words. Instead, he walked into the room—this time his footsteps were muffled by the carpet —and around the couch I was sitting on until he was standing in front of me. His eyes never left me.

He bent down until he was kneeling before me, and I felt my nerves go into overdrive. Ace held out his hand, welcoming me to take it. I stared at the outstretched hand for a moment before placing my shaky hand in his. He squeezed before letting go. Soon I found myself pulled into his arms and receiving the warmest embrace that I'd had in what felt like a very long time.

Neither of us said a word as we held on to each other, potentially scared that if the other let go, they would vanish into the afternoon sky. Being in his arms again was an emotional experience. Nothing that we'd done together could have prepared me for what I was feeling right now. The journey I was on had led me back here, and even though it wasn't permanent, I enjoyed this moment for what it was: my stay here would be temporary, and I would be safe from the assholes who were determined to get me.

Ace pulled away first. I immediately missed the comfort Ace's arms provided. His hand caressed my cheek as his eyes centered on mine once more. His stare moved to my lips and his thumb ran across them. I opened my mouth slightly, confused by what this might mean. I wondered what his next move was going to be.

His gaze shifted to my eyes before returning to my lips. His head moved closer to mine and instinctively my eyes closed. The touch of his lips on mine, once again, crossed a line that I didn't know existed. When his lips touched mine for the first time, I was shocked. Tonight, this felt so much more potent because I'd anticipated it. His kisses were something I could easily become addicted to. Now I knew what he meant when he said kissing felt more intimate.

He applied more pressure to our kiss and a sense of urgency came over me. I needed to get him as close to me as possible and quickly. When he pulled away, I groaned.

"I tried to avoid kissing you for so long for a myriad of reasons." He stroked my hand, comforting me with a simple gesture.

"I noticed." The comment came out snappier than intended. The nerves that I felt from being back here melted away from one kiss. I wanted him with the same amount of urgency that he'd just shown me. What I didn't mention was how much it hurt me that he'd never kissed me until now, but I didn't need to. The look in his eyes was enough to tell me he knew.

When he said nothing in response, I continued. "We have so much to talk about." I was stating the obvious, although I didn't really want to talk right now.

"I know," he said, but he didn't stop stroking my back. The comfort it provided was unmatched by anything I could dream of.

"I'm terrified."

"I know," he repeated. "Soon that feeling will pass, because there's nothing you need to worry about while you're here with me."

Any false belief that I had that this would only be a case of him protecting me was removed. There was something else here, something I was afraid to investigate further because of the tornado of emotions I felt.

"We have plenty to discuss, but I don't think I can handle talking about it right now. All I want is you. I want you to wash away all the pain and fear that I felt over the last few days. The only thing that I want to think about is you."

"I have no problem providing that." He leaned toward me and kissed me, connecting our bodies once again. I wanted to know why he'd deprived us of this feeling, but I knew he had to come to me with that information, and I couldn't just demand it. I was willing to wait and be patient with him.

"Let's go," he said.

We both stood up and he wrapped an arm around me. Together, we walked out of the living room and into the hallway. I didn't see Anderson or Marnie as we walked together up the stairs and down the hallway. We stopped at the door just before the guest room I stayed in.

My confusion must have appeared on my face because Ace smirked before opening the door to his bedroom. The only time I'd seen what was in there was in the brief moments that the door between our rooms was open.

The walls were a light gray and while the furniture was black, it struck a delicate balance with the lightness of the wall. It differed from the feel of the rest of the house, which I mostly associated with being dark and dreary. A darker-gray comforter covered the bed, and I noticed a picture frame on the night table.

I walked over to it, and he said nothing as I picked it up and studied the photo. It was obvious that it had been taken decades ago and had a photo of a woman sitting on a porch with a young boy on her lap. Both were smiling widely for the photo.

"Is this you and your mom?"

Ace walked over to me and took the photo out of my hand. "It is. I found the photo while you were here and put it up." He put it back down on the night table.

It left me trying to find something else to say. I didn't want to say the wrong thing and screw up him cracking the door to his past. "This room looks different from the rest of the house." There. That was much more neutral.

"It was one of the few things I changed to make it homier for me."

I nodded and expected him to lead me toward the bed once he closed the door, instead he headed to another door.

"Where are you going?"

"To draw us a bath."

I did a double take. "Seriously?"

"Yes. Did you think I was just going to toss you on the bed and fuck you?"

I stared at him blankly.

He shook his head. "There might be times that will happen, but tonight is different. I'm here to wash away the thoughts of what you've been through."

I nodded slowly, not sure I believed that this was my reality.

"We're doing things a little differently tonight. Trust me."

16

ACE

The look on her face when we entered my bathroom was priceless. It was another room in the house that I'd done extensive renovations on about a year ago. It included the addition of an enormous tub that I didn't get to use much, but that all would change now.

I started the bath and turned to look at Harlow. She was taking in the room around her, her eyes wide open in amazement. Good. I liked to keep her guessing and being able to surprise her with this small gesture was both a good and a bad thing. I was happy because she was happy, but it showed that few people had taken the time to spoil her. At least for tonight, she wouldn't have to worry about a thing.

Tomorrow was another day, and I would respect her desire to wait until then to talk about her demons. We stared at each other in silence as the tub filled up. I took off my jacket and loosened my tie. Her eyes were trained on me as she watched me make myself more comfortable.

"There are some bath bombs in that cabinet over there."

"You own bath bombs?"

I chuckled. "What's wrong with me having bath bombs?"

"I—uh—I just never expected you to be the type of person to own any, that's all."

"How presumptuous of you. I bought them for you initially, in case you wanted them while you were here. Since your bathroom does not have a tub, I stored them in this bathroom."

As I rolled up my sleeves, I noticed that I'd left Harlow stunned. I felt the water temperature to make sure that it was still warm, and when I confirmed it was, I stood up and Harlow was tossing a bath bomb into the water. I wasn't shocked that she'd chosen a lavender-scented bomb.

"Take off your clothes. The water is just about ready," I told Harlow as I dried my hands on the hand towel hanging on the wall near the tub.

She did as I said. I returned the favor and watched her every move. Although she'd dyed her hair, which would take me some time to get used to, her body looked almost the same. Still perfect in every way.

I watched as Harlow eased herself into the tub. She allowed her head to rest on the edge of the tub, not caring that the ends of her new dark locks were getting wet.

"Are you going to join me?"

All thoughts of asking about the change in hair color fled my mind. There was nothing more I wanted than to join her. I wasted no time undressing and soon, I, too, was easing my body behind hers. Feeling her skin upon mine for the first time in a while was euphoric, something I hadn't acknowledged that I'd been craving since the moment she'd stormed out of my home.

"When's the last time you took a bath?"

That was a safe question. I thought about it for a moment before I answered. "When I tested this tub out when it was installed. You?"

"Probably when I was sixteen or seventeen. Mama Robinson told me it was an excellent way to ease my sore muscles after I did a three-mile run. That was before I really got into swimming."

"You seem to be very fond of her."

"She was amazing. Losing her rocked my entire life in a bad way. She'd adopted me several years before she passed, and although we didn't have much, what we had was magical. I knew she would go to the ends of the earth for me, and I would do the same for her. Hence, the whole fiasco with Falcone."

This simple conversation with Harlow painted a better picture of her in my mind. Here was a young woman who was a protector and would do anything to help those she cared about. But who was there to take care of her?

I was. I was the person who was going to take care of her.

And right now, I was doing just that. A soothing bath in the middle of the day was out of the norm, but necessary for her well-being. The way she'd laid her head on my chest and sighed while I drew small circles on her stomach soothed me. It was relaxing for her based on the soft sighs that left her lips every so often as we sat here in a newfound silence.

I moved my hand from her stomach and played with the new, darker, wet strands that caressed her shoulders. "Why'd you dye your hair?"

"Because I was in hiding and thought no one would think that I would change my appearance. Plus, I wanted a change."

"It looks fantastic on you."

She chuckled. "Hardly. A woman I met in the house I was staying in helped me to dye my hair. It's not the best job, but it did the trick. I want to get it fixed eventually but—"

"No buts. If you want to get it fixed, we'll make it happen."

Harlow leaned forward a bit and looked back at me over her shoulder.

"If I said no, you wouldn't take it for an answer, anyway."

"I told you before, I wouldn't force you to do anything you didn't want to do. So if you don't want to go to a hairdresser, you won't have to."

That answer seemed to appease her because she settled back down against my chest.

We spent the rest of the bath in peaceful silence, and when Harlow was ready to get out, I exited first, grabbed a towel off of the towel warmer, and quickly dried myself off before tying the towel around my waist. I helped her out of the tub and handed her a towel. I couldn't help but stare at her as she dried off.

The simple movements and seeing her naked body again was enough to make me want to bend her over and fuck her right here, but I refrained. Instead, I grabbed a robe for her to put on. Today was about taking care of her, not drilling her like I was a sixteen-year-old having sex for the first time. When we were both ready to leave the bathroom, we went into my bedroom. I walked over to my nightstand and grabbed a remote. I closed the curtains and turned on the lights before dimming them to create the mood I was going for. It wasn't a replica of our night at Elevate, but I hoped it was enough to provide similar vibes. I gently pushed her down onto the bed and tossed my towel to the side.

"Do you want to make up for lost time? If not, that's perfectly fine."

"We weren't separated for that long, Ace. Not to mention we've been together for a week now."

"Any time away from you is too long."

I watched as sadness crossed her face before a hint of a smile appeared. She sat there quietly for a moment before she nodded her head. "I agree."

If I could bring Ian back from the dead and murder him repeatedly, I would. I studied her face before I made my next move because I wanted to give her the opportunity to change her mind, but her expression remained firm. "Is this what you want, Harlow?"

"Yes."

My eyes landed on her lips, and I wondered how I'd gone this long without kissing her again. I knew that once I got a taste of her, I wouldn't be able to get enough. I knew her lips would be my undoing, but what I didn't expect was that her lips would remove the negative connotation I'd developed with kissing. Now I couldn't get enough.

When our lips touched, the moan that left her mouth told me she'd been looking forward to this too. I took things slower than I would normally have, taking care to not apply too much pressure. When she parted her lips, I took it as an opportunity for our tongues to meet, throwing out the idea that doing things nice and easy was the right approach. This time, a groan left my body before I could control myself.

I broke the kiss before things became too frantic and used the tips of my fingers to turn her head to the side. My lips kissed her along her jawline and down her throat. I made sure to kiss every inch that my mouth could reach before my hand took control and drifted down her body. I cupped her breasts through the robe and smiled against her neck at her quick intake of breath. My intended effect had been achieved, so I slowly moved my hand and slid it between the fabric of the robe and her bare skin. When I found her breast again, I went back to massaging her, alternating between that, and tweaking her nipples into stiff peaks. I longed to suck on her tits, but that would have to wait until I finished my mission on her neck.

When I found that spot that I knew she liked, I sucked on it, enjoying the sweet melody that her moans made in my ear. I kissed my way up her neck to her jawline and then finally to those precious lips I now couldn't get enough of. Everything about her was enticing to me and there wasn't a doubt in my mind that she was perfect for me.

A tinge of guilt about how I pushed her away appeared before I shoved it out of my memory for the time being. It was something that I would have to live with, but I couldn't focus on it now. All that mattered was fulfilling her needs and bringing her pleasure.

My mouth left a trail of kisses back down her neck until I found her breasts. I took my time, showering each one with the attention it deserved, watching as her nipples hardened under my touch. Having her body wiggling under mine in fits of ecstasy was the most beautiful sight in the world.

But the fun was just beginning.

I drifted down her body, making sure that I continued to leave a path of kisses. When I reached her pussy, I heard her gasp before I touched her. The anticipation of her cunt in my mouth was almost too much for me to handle as well.

"You're not allowed to touch me while I fuck you with my tongue. Got it?"

She moaned in response, and I wasn't sure if she heard me or not. There were a multitude of ways to find out, but I knew which one would be the most fun. I allowed my fingertips to lightly touch her, teasing her instead of giving her what she wanted. I watched as she squeezed the sheets between her fingers, trying to avoid giving in to her desire to push my head to her pussy.

"You're so wet already, sweetness."

I watched her swallow hard as she tried to keep herself together and I couldn't help but smile. I'd waited long enough, denying her something she so desired.

When I finally gave in, a mixture of a sigh and a moan left her lips. Her arousal was enough to send me into overdrive. I allowed my tongue to get a taste of everything her cunt had to offer.

"It's a sin that I've been denied your pussy for so long."

When she groaned again, my patience snapped. Teasing her meant I was also denying myself and I couldn't take it anymore. Having her, all of her, was the only priority I had, and my mouth descended on her again, this time with no mercy. I couldn't stop and I knew it was killing her to not run her hands through my hair while I feasted on her. I didn't let up, determined to bring her as close to the edge as possible. The noises encouraged me to speed up my tactics because I knew it was only a matter of time before she would careen off the edge.

"I-I'm going to—"

"You're going to come on my dick is what you're going to do."

In one swift motion, I pulled my mouth away from her pussy and my cock was at her entrance, eagerly waiting to join this party. I ran my dick up and down her seam, coating it in her juices. Before she could take another breath, I was buried inside her and my eyes flew shut as I embraced the feeling of her pussy's grip on me.

I gave her the opportunity to adjust to me before I moved again. If she ever tried to leave me again, I would go to the ends of the earth to find her and remind her of this very moment. What it's like between us when we get together like this.

"You should see the way your pussy swallows my cock whole."

I slowly moved against her and could see that she was growing more agitated. Her eyes opened and met mine, but I wanted to take this slower than what we'd become accustomed to because of what she'd been through.

"Ace."

The raspiness in her voice caught my attention. I stopped moving as I waited for her to continue.

"Stop treating me like I'm fragile, like glass. Fuck. Me."

Everything else flew out of my mind and primal need set in. I needed to own her in every way possible. The need to consume her was enough to make me growl.

I never thought I wanted children of my own, but she'd flipped that and many of the things I thought I wanted on its head. Why had that thought entered my mind?

There was no time to dissect that right now, but it answered something for me. It was then that I decided that this first time in a while wasn't going to be easygoing. No, I'd set out to prove a point that no one touched what was mine and if I had to mark her as a reminder, so be it. My body moved again on its own, setting a pace that went from soft motions to determined and driven strokes with the sole purpose of making sure I fucked her hard enough that she would never forget who made her feel like this.

The sounds of our bodies coming together as one was erotic as fuck. It was one I would never tire of, and I hoped to hear that sound for the rest of my life.

Harlow's cry out as she flew over the edge was like lightning striking my body. I fucked her through her orgasm until I reached my own, sending us both off into a bliss that neither one of us ever wanted to come back from.

17

HARLOW

My eyes fluttered open and the realization of what happened last night flowed to the surface. I smiled because last night was magical, but I knew the real test would come today. There was so much that needed to be discussed. Who knew where we would end up once we were on the other side?

When I stretched my body to prepare to get up, I suddenly stopped moving. It was then I noticed that there was an arm slung across my stomach. I reached down and lightly grazed the hairs on his arm with my finger. I slowly flipped my body over because this wasn't something I wanted to miss. The last time I'd gotten to watch him sleep had been marred by a nightmare he'd had, and I wanted to replace it with this memory.

It looked as if last night had taken more out of him than he let on, and I couldn't stop giggling.

"What are you laughing about?" His voice was deeper in the morning, and I loved the sound of it.

"That you're still lying in bed with me. Didn't expect you to still be here when I woke up."

"I'm a morning person so I'm usually on the go." One of his eyes popped open and focused on me. Between that and the soft smirk on his face, I couldn't help but chuckle. Since when did I become the woman who giggled around a man?

"What do you have to do today?"

"You."

I rolled my eyes playfully. "Seriously."

"Spending the day with you. We can have as much time as you need to discuss everything we need to talk about."

"But your job—"

"Can wait. I have staff in place that can handle everything, and if there is an emergency, they will contact me. Let's get some food in our bodies and then we can take this conversation wherever you want."

Ace tightened his grip on my waist before letting me go. I opted to give my body the full, proper stretch it needed after last night's activities and turned to find a small smile on his face.

"This is a beautiful sight, especially first thing in the morning."

I could feel my cheeks heating. It was something else that I wasn't used to. The effect that he had on me made me giddy.

"Did you want to shower together?"

"As if I want to do it any other way now."

I stopped myself before another giggle left my lips. I was the happiest I had been in a while. This felt like one of those relationships you only saw in a movie. Yes, I was worried about the future and what might come of everything that I was involved in, but right now, I focused on spending another intimate moment with Ace.

He got out of bed first and dug around in his bag. Then he walked over to my side with his hand stretched out. I took the opportunity to look at his bare body. Neither one of us had bothered getting dressed last night because it would only have been a barrier. We both wanted the least amount of obstacles possible.

"There are some things I forgot to give you."

Ace handed me the smartphone and the credit card he'd given me when we were together last time.

"I knew this wouldn't have gone over well if I'd given it to you before today."

I nodded because he was right. "What are we going to do about the flip phone I had while I was hiding?"

"Keep it in case Emma tries to contact you. I doubt she will, but it doesn't hurt to have it."

I placed the phone and the credit card on the bedside table. Ace helped me out of bed and together we walked into the bathroom. I waited while he turned the shower on.

It didn't take long for us to get thoroughly soaked from the shower. It did not surprise me to find my favorite body wash, shampoo, and conditioner were already in there. I grabbed the shampoo bottle and smiled at the familiar scent that wafted through the air before I worked the liquid into my hair. When I felt Ace's hands join mine, I stopped massaging the shampoo into my scalp. He took over and I leaned into his motions, happy to let him take the lead. When he was done, I rinsed out my hair, added the condi-tioner, and began washing my body with the body wash. His hands made their way to my shoulders, determined to give them a massage before stopping at my breasts.

I watched as his hands cupped them before rubbing his index fingers across my nipples. The water that was raining down on me added another sensation to the effect he was having on me.

"You can't be ready to go again. We just did it like two hours ago." And several hours before that as well. Ace took the rest of the evening off, and a marathon of passionate sex had taken us through the night. It was as if we were making up for lost time and I didn't mind that one bit.

"You make me insatiable, sweetness."

As much as the nickname annoyed me, I had to admit that I'd missed it when I'd taken off. It started out as something that annoyed me and grew into something more, and I wasn't sure when it had happened.

"You're doing this on purpose," I said.

"Doing what?"

"You know exactly what."

He leaned down until his lips met the shell of my ear. "I want to hear you say the words."

Thinking about saying the words out loud made me feel embarrassed. After what we'd done over the course of time we'd known each other, including going to a sex club, I didn't understand why.

"Come on. You can do it, baby. Tell me what I'm doing to you right now."

When he teased my nipples again, rubbing his fingers across them before lightly pinching them, I gasped.

"What am I doing to you?"

The question made me quiver and led to my nipples

becoming hard like pebbles. "You're touching my breasts and my nipples."

I could feel his cock growing harder against my back. "What do you want me to do next?"

My eyes shut as I licked my lips. I knew what I longed for him to do at this point, and I wasn't afraid to let him know. The words rushed out of my mouth. "Touch my pussy."

A light chuckle left his mouth. "What was that? I want you to repeat it nice and slow."

My eyes opened and I swallowed hard before taking a deep breath. "I want you to touch my pussy."

"With pleasure." One hand stayed on my breast while the other migrated down my body. "Spread your legs a bit."

I did as he requested and in no time, he was sliding his hand between my thighs. When he played with my folds, denying me the pleasure of what I really wanted him to do, I growled and threw my head back so that it was leaning on his shoulder.

"Fuck," he mumbled. The feeling was mutual.

"Ace?"

"Yes?"

"I want you to finger me."

He groaned and then asked, "Are you sore?"

I took a quick inventory of myself and shook my head.

"Excellent." That was what it took for him to enter me with his finger.

I sighed, finally getting what I wanted. He took his time at first, fingering me slowly before removing his finger completely.

"What?"

He didn't respond to me, instead he grabbed another

bottle that I hadn't noticed before. A quick glance showed me that it was lube. When he was done with the bottle, he put it back down and looked at me.

"You're so wet for me right now, but this is just a precaution. Bend over."

I wasted no time in doing so and he rewarded me immediately. This time he slid two fingers into me and after a few seconds, began to fuck me hard. I cried out in pleasure, basking in the glory that he was bringing me.

Any embarrassment that I felt earlier was long gone as he continued to fuck me. I could feel myself growing closer and closer to the edge when he suddenly stopped and removed his fingers. Before I could voice my displeasure, one of his hands landed on my waist and I felt the head of his cock at my entrance.

"There's no way in fucking hell that I'll miss the opportunity for you to come all over my dick."

I was mid-moan when he entered me, and the air in my lungs suddenly rushed out, almost leaving me gasping for air. He gave me a second to take a deep breath before he took me. All of me. I knew once he was done, there would be nothing more of me to give him.

"What am I doing to you, Harlow?" His other hand landed on the opposite thigh, anchoring me to him.

"Fucking me."

This time, he smirked. "Good girl."

I moaned at his words.

"Do you like when I fuck you? Do you like when I praise you when you do what I tell you to do?"

"Yes!" The word left my lips followed by a yelp, and then

another groan followed because he switched positions slightly and that had changed his angle.

"I can tell you're getting close," he said gruffly.

I wasn't about to argue with him about how he knew because he was right. The harder he pumped into me, the more he was driving me wild.

"Please," I begged, not even recognizing the sound of my voice. Who was I? What was I becoming?

He grunted as I bit my lip for a second, before I realized I didn't give a damn about what sounds left my mouth. All I cared about was the pleasure he was giving me and how quickly I could orgasm.

When my orgasm crashed through me, I cried out, happy to have finally found ecstasy. That did nothing to deter him because he kept going and soon I felt him explode inside of me. I could hear the harshness of his breath over the rushing of the water from the shower and I couldn't deny it: I was proud to have driven him to such a state.

The hand that had been on my upper thigh landed on the shower wall as he tried to catch his breath. Feeling him still inside me, the connection that we shared in this very moment, was surreal. As we both tried to recover from our releases, I hoped things wouldn't be all downhill from here.

18

HARLOW

Swimming again was a joy. Outside of the library, the pool might have been my favorite place on the entire property. It gave me tranquility when my mind was in overdrive about things I didn't have full control over. And that meant talking more with Ace.

We hadn't spoken about what any of this meant. Yes, we were sleeping together, yes, I was living with him, but was this all a part of the arrangement? We hadn't mentioned it since I'd moved back in with him and it was about time we did.

When I pulled myself out of the pool, I dried myself off and tossed a robe on my body. It was getting darker earlier now and I confirmed with a glance at my phone that dinner would be served in about ninety minutes. That was still enough time to grab a snack and not completely ruin dinner.

With my things in hand, I headed to the kitchen and found Marnie cutting up some vegetables. She gave me a warm smile when I entered.

"I know dinner is soon, but I needed something to hold

me over." I grabbed an apple that she kept in a fruit basket on the counter. The vibrancy of the fruit basket did wonders for the kitchen. With the new stove and refrigerator, a warmer white on the walls, new light fixtures and countertops, the kitchen looked brand new.

"Before you go, are we still on for another cooking lesson?"

"Yes, of course! If you're still up for it."

My answer put a spark in Marnie's eye. She loved teaching me to cook and it was nice to have someone else I could talk to here.

"Would tomorrow work for you?" she asked.

"Yes. I think Ace has a meeting in the city, so he won't be here, anyway."

"Great. I'll call you both when dinner is ready."

I left the kitchen and snacked on my apple as I walked up the stairs and to the master suite. As I blow-dried my hair, I took the opportunity to further prolong the inevitable. I knew I was being a coward, but I wasn't looking forward to talking to Ace about basically everything. The conversation might become tense, but there were some things I needed to know.

I wasn't completely clear on Falcone's relationship with Ace and it was bugging me that I didn't. Knowing why he'd waited so long to kiss me was also on the list. I tried to keep most of the things that I was feeling to myself for fear of dragging someone else down with me. There was no way I could get away with that with Ace.

I turned off the hair dryer and unplugged it. When I finished putting it away, I took a deep breath and looked at myself in the mirror. It was easy to see the glow that had kissed my skin. It was amazing what being treated with kindness could do to a person. Great sex probably also had something to do with it.

I smiled at the vision of myself. I wasn't out of the woods yet by any means, but for some reason, this felt like it was the right path. Who knew where it would lead, but I would follow it until I had to make a change.

Ace: *You mentioned wanting to talk before dinner? Meet me in the living room when you're ready.*

Me: *Okay. I'll be done in a second.*

I smoothed my hands along the dark jeans I'd thrown on after my shower and left the guest bathroom. Ace and I agreed to meet down in the living room to have our talk and that was where I was headed. We agreed it would be a more neutral ground because it wasn't the bedroom, where it would be only a matter of time before one of us would want to jump the other, nor was it his office, which seemed too formal.

When I walked into the living room, I found him staring at the fireplace, a glass of red wine in his hand. I saw that he'd poured another glass for me and had been waiting for me to arrive.

I cleared my throat and he turned around, greeting me with his fiery gaze. If he'd wanted to take me right now, it would be the least surprising thing that had happened to me all week. Once he'd set his glass down and walked over to me, he pulled me into his arms. I smiled after he kissed me on the lips. He led me over to the couch, and once I was seated, he picked up my wineglass and handed it to me, before grabbing his and joining me on the sofa.

"Before you begin, there's something I wanted to say first."

I'd thought that I'd be doing most of the talking so him

wanting to speak first had caught me off guard. "What do you want to tell me?"

He squeezed my hand, and I took a sip of my wine, hoping the liquid would calm my nerves down a bit.

"I wanted to say out loud that everything related to the auction doesn't matter anymore."

"What do you mean? That was how we met and that's how I came to live here."

"And I don't give a shit about it anymore. I'm not looking for you to fulfill the ninety-day requirement. If you want to be here, I want you to be here."

"Do you want me to be here?"

I'd gone into this thinking he wanted me here temporarily, but I didn't want to end up lying to myself to make myself feel better. I thought he wanted me here the first time around, and he pulled the rug out from underneath me just before I got the hell out.

"I do and I think you need me only half as much as I need you."

My eyes widened at his comment. "You can't say that and then not continue."

He then took a sip before setting his wine down. He took my hand that wasn't holding the wineglass into his and said, "If Emma hadn't admitted to where you were, I would have gone to hell and back to make sure that I brought you back here."

"And if I didn't want to be here?"

"I never thought that would be the case. Deep down, even when I was telling you that we wouldn't be together anymore, I was lying to myself and to you because I was struggling through my own shit. I didn't think you would leave because I thought you still needed me. And you didn't."

"I needed to." My answer was short, but it was the truth. I needed to leave this place in order to find myself. I came back because I knew that this was the place where I would be the safest, as well as everyone around me. What I hadn't expected was for this place to become my sanctuary. Then it clicked. It was because he was here. The man in front of me.

Being cared for by him was a change I'd love to embrace, but it would take some time to get used to it.

"I didn't want you to be forced to be saddled with an old man."

That made me whip my head to look at him. "You're not old."

"I'm older than you."

I rolled my eyes before I realized that made me look somewhat childish. "It's still my decision to make."

"That it is. You have your whole life in front of you and deserve to live it."

"I can do that with you, Ace. Nothing you're doing is holding me back here. I'm here because I want to be. I promise."

It was the first time I could remember seeing Ace nervous. His eyes continued to search mine as if they were looking for a sign that I was lying. But I wasn't. I truly believed that being with him was what would make me happy.

Ace finally saw the answer that I'd hoped he would see. His hand tucked a small piece of my hair behind my ear, and he leaned in to kiss me, sealing our new arrangement. The kiss was intense with emotion, and I could feel a tear slowly rolling down my cheek when both of his hands landed on my face.

When he pulled away, he wiped another tear that had fallen from my other eye. "I don't want you to cry."

"It's not exactly something I can control. I'm just happy."

"And I will do everything in my power to keep it that way. Now, what did you want to ask me?"

I decided to only ask one of my questions because I knew it had to almost be dinner time. "What's your relationship with Falcone?"

"I don't have much of one. He had some business dealings with my grandfather before he retired. Why?"

"Just curious after...well everything."

Ace nodded and before he could respond, there was a knock. The sound brought our attention away from each other and to Marnie, who was standing near the door.

"Dinner is ready," she said.

19

ACE

I checked my watch, hoping this meeting would end now. I wanted to get back to Harlow as quickly as possible and this Chevalier meeting was holding me up.

She was at my house upstate with Marnie and Anderson. What she didn't know was that I also had several members of Cross Sentinel watching the home as well. Everyone besides Harlow had orders to do anything and everything to protect her at all costs. The longer I spent away from her, the more irritated I became.

I also needed to get back home and do some more prepping for the board meeting I needed to run. Being prepared for anything that someone might throw at me was of extreme importance. I refused to look weak in front of anyone, let alone them.

"Does anyone have more information that they would like to present?"

"About time," I heard the man next to me mutter.

He echoed the sentiments I felt, and I did my best to keep

my expression neutral. But when I slightly nodded my head, I caught his attention and he smirked.

"And with that, our meeting is adjourned."

The shift in tension in the room with Parker's announcement was obvious. Light murmurs filled the air, whereas seconds before, everyone was silent outside of the speaker's voice.

My phone vibrated in my pocket and when I looked at the screen, I found a message from Kingston.

Kingston: *Need to talk quickly after this.*

My eyes searched the room and found him sitting in the corner on the other side of the room. Kingston had snuck into the meeting after it had already begun and when our eyes met, I nodded at him, confirming I'd received the message.

"So, you've met Slade Walker."

I looked up and found Parker Townsend standing to my left. I stood up so that we were both at eye level. "Who?"

"The man that was sitting next to you during our business meeting."

"Ah, in this case, met is an interesting term. We were both ready for this meeting to be over. No offense to you."

"None taken. I know sometimes these meetings can be long and tedious."

"Is he someone I should know about?"

"Potentially? He moved here from California after making his mark in the tech world. It wouldn't be a terrible connection to have. But we can talk about him later."

I nodded. "I assumed that isn't why you came over to chat."

Parker leaned toward me and whispered, "Did you find anything interesting in that packet I gave you?"

"I did. Thank you. There is one thing that I don't understand, though."

He shifted his stance and crossed his arms. "What's that?"

"Why did you give me that information?"

"There are things that you don't know, and I hoped what I found would bring some clarity."

I rolled his words around in my head for a moment before I asked, "What is it you're not telling me?"

"Why do you think I'm not telling you something?"

"Because you deflected my question with a question."

Parker's smirk confirmed my suspicions. "I've already given you the tools. It's up to you to decide if you want to keep digging and if you want to find all the answers. I have kept many of them buried for a reason."

"You mean like the line items referencing Falcone and a 'KH'?"

"Excuse me, chairman?"

The question from another member of the Chevaliers stopped our conversation. He was someone I'd seen once or twice during our meetings, so I chalked it up to him being a newer member or someone who had recently transferred to this alumni chapter.

Before either of them could say something else, I stuck my hand out to shake Parker's hand. "I'll see you later."

He returned my handshake and I nodded at both men before I left. I needed to take another look at those papers.

"Ace." I turned toward the sound of the familiar voice. "Did you drive down here?"

"No, I hired a driver. Why?"

"I'll ride back with you to your place and catch a ride back to the city with my men."

I raised an eyebrow at him. "That's going out of your way."

"We need to debrief, and Ellie is away on a girls' trip with Anais, so I'm not going home to anyone."

"Ah, so you're trying to stay busy."

Kingston shrugged. "Something like that."

We made our way out of the Chevaliers headquarters and to my driver's car. I pulled the divider up between the back seat and the driver's seat.

"What did you want to talk about, Kingston?"

"I had several updates for you on the shit we've been tracking down."

We hit a pothole, causing both Kingston and me to jump slightly. "Good or bad?"

"Can 'not great' be an option?"

Shit. "Sure. Tell me what you know."

Kingston ran a hand across his face before he began. "Remember when I called you and told you that Falcone knew you killed Ian?"

I recalled when Kingston called me right after Harlow and I arrived at my home outside of the city. That's when he delivered the news that Falcone had found out about Ian, but we didn't know when he found out or how long it took to leak the news.

"That's all we have. Falcone hasn't made a peep since, which is unusual. Once Will's men started getting close, he disappeared."

I feared that would happen. When I saw the news story about the murder outside of Bar 53, it made sense for

Falcone to eventually go underground to protect his own ass. The fact he didn't do it sooner was more telling. What was the deciding factor in making him run away scared now? Hell, I might never find out why. "I imagine Will is pissed."

"And I know you are too."

He was right. I wasn't happy because I knew it made Falcone more dangerous. If he'd sent Ian after Harlow, he could be gearing up for another assault, especially since Ian didn't succeed and was now dead.

"Are you working with Will to keep an eye out for Falcone?"

Kingston dipped his head. "We have so many eyes and ears on the ground that the moment he surfaces, we will have him. I promise you that."

I trusted Kingston's words. "Is there anything else?"

"A couple of more things. We found out more information about Emma. We suspect she skipped town but we are following up on a couple of leads. 'Emma' is just another name in a list of aliases that she has used in various places over the years. In fact, at one point, someone enrolled her into Brentson High a few years back."

That triggered a memory from the case that Kingston had asked me to investigate in the latter part of summer, only a couple of weeks before Harlow had come into my life. "Did she know your half sister?"

He shrugged. "I know they were in high school at the same time, but whether they knew each other is still up in the air."

"Do we have her real name?"

"Mary Horne. Originally from Delaware. She kept her

correct age but would change her physical features if necessary when moving to a new place to run a grift."

"Any family that we can track down? Maybe she went back to them."

Kingston nodded. "Her father is still in Delaware, and we have a tail on him in case she shows up there or he tries to leave. While we are covering all of our bases, supposedly, she is with Falcone."

That was an interesting development after what Emma told Harlow. "But that would directly contradict what Harlow told us the evening we rescued her. When I handed off that money to you, she said Emma supposedly stole it from Falcone."

"True, but we don't know if it might have been a preemptive setup so that Falcone and Ian knew where Harlow was and then they both waited a bit before striking. Thankfully, we got there when we did."

He could say that again. "So now we have both Falcone and Emma in the wind."

"Right, which makes things more dangerous for both you and Harlow."

I didn't respond right away. It took me some time to digest his words and I wondered what my next move should be. "I might need to employ some more of your guys for the time being. I can protect myself, but if moments like this evening where I'm called away on business, I want Harlow to be protected."

"Understandable and you know we are ready to help you and protect her."

I tapped my fingertips on my knee when an idea came to

me. "You know what? It might not be such a bad idea to escape the city for a while."

Kingston swung his head to look at me. "I agree, but since when do you go on vacation?"

"Since now. I'll make plans for Harlow and me to leave town and hopefully we'll have some more information on Falcone and Emma by the time we return."

20

———

HARLOW

I enjoyed it when I lay on him. Listening to his heart beating in my ear was soothing. Here, in this bed, we could forget about our demons and just enjoy one another.

He'd come home after some meeting in the city and together we entered the master suite and fell asleep. The clock on his bedside table said that we'd been sleeping for a few hours before I woke up in the middle of the night, unable to fall back to sleep.

"You should go back to sleep," he mumbled, his voice deeper than normal.

"Sorry if I woke you up."

"Don't worry, I'll make you pay for it."

He stretched slightly, making me giggle when the hair on his chest lightly brushed my cheek because of his movements. My laughter turned into a gasp when he flipped us over.

"I dreamed about eating your sweet pussy again and I'm about to make it a reality."

Before I could take my next breath, Ace had slid down my body and was eye level with my pussy. His fingers wasted no time and began playing with my clit. I bit my lip as I watched him work me into a frenzy.

He took things a step further and I groaned in delight. Ace ran a teasing finger around my clit before placing his finger inside of me. He stayed there for a moment, allowing me to adjust to the intrusion before his finger moved. When he built up a pace that had me almost ready to ride his hand, he used his tongue to flick my clit. I couldn't fight the shiver that passed through my body. I gasped when he added another finger.

When Ace did it a second time, I moaned and then his mouth attacked my pussy with a vigor I'd never seen before. My eyes closed as I allowed the sensations to take over. When I cried out, my voice reached a higher pitch that I'm sure would have sounded quite comical any other time, but neither of us cared in this moment.

Ace moved his mouth for a moment and said, "Fucking come for me, sweetness. I want to feel your pussy clamp down on my fingers."

That was all it took. The hurricane that tore through my body was almost too much to bear, but I couldn't be happier.

"I think my payback fits the crime, don't you think?"

I barely heard his question over the pounding in my ears. He was very pleased with himself, but I didn't care. My main priority was stabilizing my breath. When my breathing slowed, I couldn't think of a response. How could it be this good every time?

"I can't get enough of you. This wasn't supposed to be this way."

I opened my eyes and looked at him. "What do you mean?" I wrapped the sheet around myself and waited for him to respond.

"I thought I would have my fill of you and then we would go our separate ways. But the desire to have you increases tenfold every time I touch you."

The feeling was mutual. We haven't discussed what any of this meant, but the pull that existed between us made it hard to stay away. Even when I fled his home, the urge to come back was there and I wondered if it would ever go away. I still wasn't sure exactly what he wanted besides me in the present. It could mean that we have a future together or it could mean that we don't. But all that mattered right now was me as I lay on his chest once more, enjoying how his body felt next to mine.

An idea popped into my head that I acted on before I could stop myself. "If you could have anything in this world, what would it be?"

"That's a very broad question."

"Humor me, Ace."

"You."

I chuckled and rolled my eyes. "Seriously."

"I don't kid, remember that. Well, now that I can buy whatever I want, but that wasn't always the case. If I had the opportunity now, I would go back in time and tell my younger self that everything would get better."

"What happened if you don't mind me asking?"

"Losing my mother when I was young was difficult."

I sat up and leaned my head on my hand, determined to give him my undivided attention.

"I could only imagine what it was like to lose a parent so

young. While I did struggle in foster care and until Mama Robinson adopted me, I never knew my mother, so I didn't understand what I was missing. However, I do sometimes wonder if she's alive and what she's done with her life since giving me up."

"Have you tried to search for her?"

"I did once and came to a dead end. I could have kept trying, but I chickened out. I was worried that she wouldn't want to meet me, so I thought, *What's the use in trying anymore?*"

I shifted my body and brushed my brown hair out of my eyes. It wasn't something I thought I would admit to anyone, let alone him, but it was funny how things changed.

I ran my hand down his chest and said, "We have a lot more things in common than I thought."

"I guess we do."

There was something bugging me about what he'd said, and I couldn't stop myself from asking him to clarify. "What did you mean about your mom being only part of the problem?"

"My grandfather was the other part."

I recalled the conversation I had with Marnie about Ace's upbringing and how she was hesitant to say too much. What she did say was that his mother's best friend took Ace in instead of his grandfather. Marine didn't go any further, but I had been curious about why that was the case.

"What did your grandfather do?"

Ace stared up at the ceiling instead of answering my question. I shifted my gaze away from him because staring at him while he didn't answer my question would increase the tension between us and make things more awkward. If he didn't want to answer the question, I would respect it. If he wanted to take his time answering the question, he was allowed to do that too.

"My grandfather barely acknowledged me when I was growing up. He kicked my mother out when he found out she was pregnant, and she did all she could to provide the best life for me that she could. She had some money from when my grandmother died, but she worked and did the best she could with what she had. She told me that if anything ever happened to her, that her best friend was prepared to take me in. And her best friend did. I assume she made those arrangements because she assumed her father would want nothing to do with me since he hadn't when she was alive."

"Is your grandfather still alive now?"

Ace nodded. "I mentioned before that he sold me the house and moved to his private island because he wanted to retire. He became more a part of my life when I was about eighteen and entering college so he could groom me to be his successor. Which is why I'm where I am today. And now that I've talked your ear off, it's time that we both go to sleep."

I wanted to ask more, but thought it was best to not poke him too much. I was happy that he'd shared what he did, but nothing he said really stood out to me as something that Marine couldn't have shared with me. Which made me wonder if there was more to his story.

WHEN I WOKE up the following day, I reached over and couldn't find Ace. I'd hoped he would still be in bed so that we could cuddle some more, but that wasn't in the cards.

After shaking my head at the silly pun I'd made, I removed the covers from my naked body. I felt slightly sore from our activities the evening before, but I wouldn't complain about it for a second. Between the hot sex and the connection between us that seemed to develop daily, what more could I possibly want?

Love.

Stability.

Deep down, I wished Ace could give me that, but with everything else going on, I didn't have the energy to approach the subject. I made my way to the bathroom, naked as the day I was born, and quickly slipped on the robe that I'd hung up in the bathroom the day before and began washing my face. As I was patting my face dry, I saw something move out of the corner of my eye and found Ace standing in the doorway.

"Hey," I said with a small smile on my face. I turned toward the mirror and looked at him through it so that I could continue getting ready. When I looked down to grab my moisturizer, I bit my lip when I heard him walk toward me. As I was putting the liquid on my face, I felt his arms wrap around my waist and he slowly undid the belt on my robe. When it fell open, my arms landed by my sides and I watched as he slowly eased the robe off of my shoulders and it fell to the floor. His gaze scorched me through the mirror and his touch was no better. When his hands made their way to my breasts, I sighed and let him have his way with me. His touch was too much to resist.

"I'm addicted to you, Harlow," he said against the shell of my ear, sending a shiver down my spine.

When he laid a small kiss on my neck and his hands squeezed my breasts simultaneously, goose bumps appeared on my skin. I knew it wouldn't take much to convince him to move his hands farther south.

"How long would it take you to pack a bag, sweetness?"

My brain was caught in a fog because of his ministrations, and it took me a moment to answer. "Maybe thirty to forty-five minutes? But that's only if the clothes you bought for me are still in the closet."

"They are. And good because I want to take you somewhere for a few days. And while I'm tempted to have a quickie right now, I have bigger plans for both of us."

"Where are we going?"

This time Ace smiled. "I'll tell you on the plane, but here's a hint that will make things easier: pack warm clothes."

21

———

HARLOW

"**I**s there anything I can get you?"

I jumped at the voice, having been dragged out of my thoughts by the intrusion. The flight attendant on the plane gave me a small smile.

"Um, yes. Can I get a glass of water?"

"Of course."

After she walked away, I rubbed my face with both hands. How was this real life? Was I really sitting on this private plane?

The plane looked like something out of a movie and was larger than I'd expected it to be. This whole day had been a whirlwind. I'd gone from standing in the master bathroom at Ace's home to sitting on a plane, preparing for takeoff. I'd only been on one twice in my life, first when I'd arrived in New York City and then on a trip to Florida that it took Mama Robinson years to save up for. Never in a million years would I have expected to be traveling by private plane anywhere.

Then my eyes landed on Ace. He was busy typing away on

his computer, not paying much attention to the outside world.

"Here's your water, Ms. Robinson."

"Thank you," I said before smiling at the flight attendant.

"Mr. Bolton."

"Yes?" Ace lifted his head slightly but continued typing.

"We're ready for takeoff."

He didn't respond for a moment, instead choosing to keep typing. It didn't take but a few more seconds before he was done. "Thank you."

She gave him a small smile before walking away and then we were by ourselves once more. Ace walked over to the seat next to mine and buckled himself in.

He reached over and grabbed my hand, giving it a squeeze and before I could blink, the plane was taking off and we were leaving New York City. I grabbed Ace's hand while the plane ascended, but once we were safely cruising, I felt comfortable letting his hand go.

"Are you finally going to tell me where we are going?"

"Maybe. Kiss me and I might be tempted to."

His demand made the butterflies in my stomach spring to life. Our flight attendant could see us. When his hand caressed my cheek, my eyes fluttered closed, and his lips grazed mine. A small voice in my head whispered that this was where I was meant to be, but I brushed it aside, instead choosing to enjoy this moment for what it was and not what I hoped deep down that it would be.

When he deepened the kiss, any thoughts about us getting caught kissing flew out the window and danced with the clouds. Our kiss ended naturally, and Ace leaned his fore-head on mine. I opened my eyes and saw the pained expression on his face. Before I could ask about it, it was gone and then his eyes bore into mine.

"Is everything okay?"

"Of course it is. Why wouldn't it be?"

I didn't know, so I didn't dig any further. I moved my head back to get a better look at him. "Where are we going?"

Ace smirked. "Deer Valley, Utah. I thought you'd enjoy some time away, and we'd have plenty of options in terms of outdoor activities as well as indoor ones."

I ignored the double meaning and the look he gave me when he said 'indoor activities. Instead, my mouth dropped open. "This is so amazing. Thank you!"

The seat belts constricted my movement significantly, so hugging him was an awkward affair. But kissing him again wasn't.

When we got the all clear to move around the cabin, Ace took off his seat belt and with an outstretched hand he said, "Let me give you a tour of the plane."

I fumbled with my seat belt for a moment before I unlocked myself and placed my hand in his. With his help, I stood up and together we walked toward the back. The tour took us to the back of the plane, where I assumed there was a bedroom behind the door we were standing next to. As I took in the space, I could feel Ace staring at me.

"This is beautiful."

"I was thinking the same thing."

At his words, I looked at him and our eyes connected instantly. He wasn't looking around the room. Instead, he was staring at me.

"That was cheesy, even for you."

"What do you mean 'even for me'?"

"You're older and it slips out sometimes."

"Oh really? When has anything I've done or said to you 'slipped out'?"

My heart skipped a beat. Just one small look from him could warm me from the inside out. I couldn't take my eyes off of him and waited to see what he would say next.

"Take your hair down."

The look in his eyes was enough to keep me mesmerized, let alone the way his voice caressed my skin. I swallowed hard as I removed my hand from his and moved both hands toward my head. When I let my hair down and shook it, he growled under his breath.

"That's a good girl."

An involuntary gasp left my lips. I could always count on his praise making me wet.

"I have some work to do."

I tilted my head slightly. "What do you mean? I thought you finished working before you gave me a tour of the plane?"

"This type of work is more personal in nature." He took his fingers and lifted my chin so that there was no mistaking where I was looking. "I have something else I want you to experience."

And his expression turned downright sinful as he descended on me.

"I assume you've never experienced what it's like to join the mile-high club."

"You'd be correct in that assumption. I've only been on an airplane a handful of times."

"Then I can't wait to take you on this journey. I want you to head into the bedroom, get completely naked and wait for me. There's something waiting for you on the bed. You have five minutes."

I stared at him for a moment, wondering if he was kidding. Then again, Ace, rarely, if ever, cracked a joke. I debated putting up a fight, but we both knew it would be bullshit because I wanted this as much as he did.

I waited as Ace turned the doorknob and let me into the room. When he closed the door behind me, my mouth dropped open.

I grabbed the small black bag sitting on the king-size bed and looked inside. There was a blindfold and nothing else.

I must have wasted a minute just staring at everything in the room. At least it wouldn't take me four minutes to get naked. I removed my clothes and stared at the blindfold before sitting down on the edge of the bed. With a deep breath, I secured the blindfold over my eyes and shifted my body back so that I could lie on the bed comfortably.

And then I waited. A moment of turbulence caused my heart to jump, and I wondered where Ace was. He'd said I had five minutes. Was time not up yet?

As if he heard my thoughts, I heard a light click. I knew Ace had walked into the room. The air rushed out of me as I wondered what he might do next.

"You don't know how beautiful you look lying there, not knowing what I might do to that delectable body of yours."

I shivered and it wasn't from a chill.

"If you have an issue with anything that is going on, I want you to say 'lavender.'"

"Why 'lavender'?"

"Because that's your favorite scent."

He was right. Most of the hygienic products bought were lavender scented.

"Hold your hand out."

I followed his directions and felt him put something in my hand.

"Those are earplugs. Put them on."

"You're blocking my sight and hearing?" What kind of game was this?

"Do you trust me, Harlow?"

I knew there was a double meaning behind his words, but I took what he said at face value. "Yes."

"Then do what I say. I believe you're in for a real treat and if there is something you don't like, what do you say?"

"Lavender."

"Good girl."

That familiar warmth that appeared whenever he applauded something I did grew. I squeezed my thighs together so as not to give my secret away.

"You know, we have something to celebrate."

I sat up to put the earplugs in my ears but paused when he spoke. "What are we celebrating?"

"It's been three months since you stormed into my life."

For a moment, I thought about it. Between the time I'd left Ace's home and the time I'd been in hiding, three months had passed since we'd met. "I can't believe you remembered the evening of the auction."

"This has nothing to do with the auction. I'm talking about when I saw you serving up drinks behind the bar at Bar 53. Now put the earplugs in your ears."

As I put the earplugs in, I remembered the evening he walked into Bar 53. He went down into the basement to have a meeting with Falcone. When I lay back down on the bed, the silence would normally fuel the thoughts in my head to creep up again because my brain didn't like to shut down. Now, there was nothing on my mind other than what Ace would do next.

It didn't take long for my question to be answered.

I felt something brushing up against my lips. Something cool and wet. It took me half a second to pinpoint the smell.

"Strawberries," I mumbled under my breath.

I must have gotten the answer right because Ace pushed some of the fruit into my mouth, allowing me to take a bite. Ace continued to feed me the fruit until I finished eating. Then he stepped away and soon something else was dancing on my lips.

"Pineapple," I announced almost immediately.

He rewarded me once again by allowing me to eat the piece of fruit and then I waited for what was next.

I felt the bed dip near my feet and based on the movements, it seemed like Ace was crawling up my body. I adjusted my head, intending to smell the next food, but he switched it up.

A gasp fell from my lips when I felt some type of liquid hit my skin, sliding across my left breast just before Ace's lips followed suit. I groaned as he licked every last drop before sticking my nipple in his mouth. When he repeated the same thing with my right breast, my body nearly bucked off the bed as I tried to get closer to his mouth.

When he paused his ministrations, I was breathing hard as I wondered what he was going to do next. It didn't take long for me to find out because he'd buried his face in my pussy, feasting on me as if this was the last thing he would ever do. The shock wore off quickly and my fingers found their way into his hair, anchoring him to my body.

It felt as if I was having an out-of-body experience and the pressure within me continued to build. It didn't take long for my breathing to become harsher and for me to explode all over his tongue.

I couldn't tell how loud I was being. Frankly, it didn't matter.

Suddenly, Ace plucked the earplugs out of my ears. "Take the blindfold off and flip over."

I did as he asked and waited for my next instructions.

But none came.

Instead, Ace grunted as he grabbed a fistful of my hair and pulled my head back. He looked me in the eye before he slammed into me. I cried out in ecstasy. I didn't care who on this plane could hear me.

The pace he kept was relentless. His tantalizing teasing had done its job because between it and him fucking me, my body was soon spinning out of control as I rode my second orgasm. He grunted as I came, but continued pounding into me until he, too, found his release.

As he was cleaning me up with a warm washcloth, he said, "I mauled you before we could have an actual meal."

My stomach growled in response, and he chuckled.

"We need to get you into the shower. I'll make sure you get some food before we land. There should be a fruit plate with more strawberries included."

I smiled up at him and said, "Perfect."

22

HARLOW

I woke up the next morning with a long stretch and got out of one of the softest beds I'd ever slept in. I'd already told Ace that we needed one for the master bedroom and he told me that he'd think about it.

But there was a smirk on his face.

Speaking of Ace, he wasn't in the bed. I assumed he probably ended up in the living room or spare office to get some work done for the board meeting that was coming up.

I tossed on one of the robes that had been left for us in the home and walked out into the living area. Ace wasn't there, so I checked the office and found him sitting at the desk typing on his computer. He stopped typing when he heard me enter the room.

"Hey, don't forget you're also on vacation, Ace."

Ace chuckled. "I know, but things need to get done."

"What are we doing today?"

"I'll be working while you're gone."

I raised an eyebrow at him. "What do you mean 'while I'm gone'?"

"I've planned some things for you to do today that I know you'll enjoy. Everything has been organized so you don't need to worry about a thing. All you have to do is get ready and walk out the door."

I stared at Ace for a moment, surprised by his answer. "What am I doing?"

"Do you trust me?"

I tossed the question around in my mind before I nodded. "Yes."

"Then all you need to know is that you'll have a lovely time today and I'll see you when you get back."

"Okay, thank you."

I couldn't deny that I was excited. I leaned over and gave Ace a deep kiss on his lips before I left the room to get ready for my day.

"YOU ARE GLOWING."

I smiled at the woman who'd been working on my hair for the last couple of hours. A spur-of-the-moment decision led me to get my brown hair fixed by a professional, bringing my hair color closer to a dirty blonde than the light brown it had been. It had been an excellent idea for my mental health and was the cherry on top of what was an amazing vacation.

I could see what she meant as I examined my freshly done hair. I ran my fingers through and played with my strands. Looking more like I was used to looking did wonders for my self-care attempts. A visit to the spa earlier started my day of relaxation and this was a great ending.

I quickly checked out and met the car that would drive

me back to the luxurious private home we were staying in. Soon, I was whisked away and taken to where I was staying.

The crisp air greeted me as my driver opened my car door and soon I found myself standing in front of the door. I opened the door to our home away from home and found Ace sitting on the couch with a laptop.

"I feel like a brand-new woman," I announced as I entered the room. I'd wanted a day where I could be pampered, and Ace was happy to oblige. "Thank you so much for today."

I did a twirl for Ace, showing off my new hair, and he gave me a light chuckle that didn't seem to reach his eyes.

"Is there something wrong?"

Ace shook his head. "Why would there be? I'm with the most beautiful woman in the universe on vacation, enjoying every moment that we spend together away from the outside world."

I couldn't help but grin. "Let's see if you still think that after I finish cooking. I'll change into something more comfortable and meet you in the kitchen."

"That's a good plan."

I hurried upstairs and changed into a pair of leggings and a baggier sweater. When I came back into the kitchen, I found Ace staring at his laptop.

"This might be the greatest idea I've ever had or the worst."

Ace looked up from his computer at me and smirked. "Does it count if I'm excited no matter how it turns out?"

"Thanks for the vote of confidence."

He shrugged. "Any time." And then his eyes were back on the screen in front of him.

For our second to last evening in Deer Valley, I decided I would cook dinner for the two of us. It might be a bit of an adventure, but since I'd been taking lessons from Marnie, I thought I would try to give it a shot on my own.

And now as I was looking at the ingredients for the lemon chicken piccata set out in front of me, I was wondering if I bit off more than I could chew. Pun intended.

I pulled my ponytail tighter and got to work on preparing the meal.

I felt him before I heard him. The feel of his body up against mine while I pounded the chicken felt sensual in a way I wasn't expecting. Then again, I was wishing this was him fucking me from behind while I leaned over the dining room table. What had having sex with Ace turned me into? This was a weird thing to be thinking about right now, but when it came to all things with Ace, it was smart to expect the unexpected.

His warm breath tickled the shell of my ear when he whispered, "How can I help?"

I was ready to throw in the towel right there and say to hell with cooking dinner. We could have sex and order take-out, all the while sitting in front of the fireplace again. I bit the corner of my lip to bite back the moan I wanted to unleash. "You can cook the pasta while I prepare the chicken."

"Deal," he said before leaving several kisses on my neck. When he stepped back, I immediately missed his warmth.

This was strangely domestic and reminded me of times I would help Mama Robinson in the kitchen. But the vibe here was different. Of course, the relationship between Ace and me differed greatly from the one that I shared with Mama

Robinson, but there was still a common thread between the two. The domestic picture Ace and I were painting right now reminded me of what it felt like to have a family.

It was something I always longed for and the time that Mama Robinson and I had as a family was cut too short. When I glanced at Ace, I found him looking back at me with a small smile on his face. Was the same idea floating through his mind? There was only one way to find out.

"This seems quite domestic for us."

"I'd agree with that. But I like it, don't you?"

His answer surprised me. I hadn't expected him to admit that he was enjoying this.

"I do because I enjoy spending this time together, alone with you. It felt good to get out of the city for a bit and not have to worry about..."

"Falcone? Ian? Any of the drama surrounding them?"

"Yes, and the security risk that Falcone imposes on me. But what feels good is to have you all to myself for the time being." There I was, putting myself out there more.

"I'd agree, although preparing for this board meeting has had me distracted."

I shrugged. "You haven't been the entire time and it gave me some time to catch up on some reading."

"And we've been doing some catching up on our own in other departments as well."

I could feel my cheeks growing hot. We'd been making up for the time we lost from when I'd made my getaway from Ace's property. Most of the surfaces in this luxurious home had seen our naked bodies and I wasn't ashamed about it one bit.

I looked around the counter to see if I could find the

chicken broth that I needed for the recipe. When I couldn't find it after a quick glance, I saw it was on the highest shelf in the cabinet nearest to me. I reached up to grab it, but I couldn't quite reach it.

I felt the warmth from Ace's hand as he touched the space where my sweater had risen, while he easily reached for the box and brought it within my reach.

"Thank you," I said when I turned to look at him.

"You're very welcome."

He wasted no time and placed a small kiss on my lips. The promise of more stayed on my lips for the rest of the time we cooked together. When the food was done, we brought our plates into the living room. Sitting on the couch and enjoying the fireplace while we ate was both romantic and relaxing.

"This is delicious, Harlow. Thank you."

I thought that his praise for me when we were having sex could get me off in a heartbeat. Having him compliment me on something I was self-conscious about made me feel like I was floating on cloud nine.

If you had asked me if this was how I thought my relationship with Ace would have turned out when we first met, I would have called you a liar. This was more than I ever could have thought of, and I hoped that what we had would never end.

23

ACE

The most I'd felt at peace had been with Harlow beside me. As she slept peacefully in my arms while the fireplace roared in front of us. Harlow and I had enjoyed an eventful day on the slopes and in the time that I've known her, I've never seen her as happy as she was today.

That made all of this worth it to me.

Sure, I would have to double down on the work I needed to do for this upcoming board meeting when we returned but seeing her light up the way she had while we'd been here could best be described as magical.

The bubble we were in wouldn't last forever, but I knew I would take my time treasuring the memories we created here.

I picked up my phone and found a missed phone call from my grandfather. I'd find the time to deal with him later. I didn't care for the man, but ever since I'd gotten those papers from Parker, something had been bothering me about him even more. While Harlow was at the spa yesterday, I looked over the papers again and couldn't find anything new. I knew I was missing something, but what I wasn't sure.

Knowing my grandfather, he was calling me because of the board meeting, but I wasn't worried about that right now. I would continue working on my presentation and making sure that my team stayed on task, but there were more important things to worry about than a board meeting.

I'd made sure that I focused mostly on her throughout this trip. When we had some downtime, I would do a few things I needed to do for work but made sure it didn't take away from the time we were supposed to spend together. The balance that we'd struck here was perfect and I'd never seen Harlow more relaxed.

I mentally recalled the conversations that I had with Kingston, thinking about how I was going to approach this with Harlow. She needed to know what was going on. She deserved to know.

"What are you thinking about?"

I'd been so caught up in my own thoughts, I hadn't realized that Harlow had woken up.

My hand felt like it weighed a ton as I brought it to my head to run my fingers through my hair. "There's been some things weighing on my mind. Things I've been keeping to myself that you should know. Because it's not fair to you to be kept in the dark."

Worry crossed her features and I felt bad about putting it there. The reasons why I'd kept these things from her were because I thought I was protecting her and opening up about my past exposed my vulnerability, but not telling her was a deterrent to both of us.

Harlow sat up on the couch and stared up at me. We were

leaving to go back to New York City tomorrow and it was time to rip the Band-Aid off.

"We haven't found Falcone or Emma yet. Hell, Emma isn't her real name."

"Do we know what her real name is?"

"Mary Horne. Some intel we have said she might be with Falcone, but we haven't been able to confirm or deny that yet. Both are MIA. The last time I saw Falcone was when I stopped by Bar 53 trying to find Emma because I needed to find you."

"What do we do now?"

That was the question of the hour. "For now, we let Cross Sentinel do their jobs and we will keep you safe."

"What would that entail?"

"I'll keep you informed about any changes, but know that no matter where you are, there is someone watching you. We also have people looking out for Emma and Falcone so whenever they resurface, we'll know."

"Okay."

"But there's more I wanted to say."

Harlow tilted her head. "Go on."

This I couldn't stay seated for. I stood up and paced back and forth twice before I found myself in the far corner of the room, looking out at the beautiful landscape that sat before us.

"I mentioned my grandfather before and you saw the picture frame of my mother and me from when I was a child."

"Yes, I remember."

"My grandfather refused to take me in when my mother, his daughter, died. So I went to live with my mother's best friend. Things were okay at first and it took some time for both of us to adjust to losing my mom."

I glanced over my shoulder and watched as tears formed in Harlow's eyes while she listened to my story. Little did she know, it was only going to get worse.

I turned back to the window before I continued. "Things took a turn and my mother's best friend wanted me to fulfill her needs. She sexually abused me for years until my grandfather eventually swooped in when I was on my way to college."

"No. Oh my—" Harlow's words died on her lips as she looked at me and shook her head in horror.

"I didn't tell anyone about how she made me sleep in bed with her or forced me to kiss her regularly."

"Is that why you refused to kiss me?"

I slowly nodded. "It was one thing she loved to do which turned me off it. That is, until I met you."

I ran a hand through my hair and turned around to finally face the woman who had flipped my world on its head. She'd stood up and I knew it was time for me to say the last thing I'd kept to myself for way too long.

"I'm admitting all of this because I love you and I don't want this standing between us."

Harlow's eyebrows shot up as her eyes widened. She jumped to her feet and exclaimed, "You do?"

"Yes. I'd prove it all to you, again and again, if that is what would make you happy. Whatever it is, the only thing I want to do is see you smile."

"I could only imagine how difficult it was for you to say all of this. For lack of a better thing to say, I want to tell you how thankful I am that you trusted me with this."

"And I—"

Harlow shook her head and walked over to me. "I wasn't finished talking. I'd hoped that this was where we were leading, but there's always a chance that something could slip away, and I didn't want to get my hopes up."

Before she could say something else, I pulled her into my arms, giving her a tight hug. "And I didn't help things when I said I wanted to end our arrangement."

She nodded against my chest. When she shifted her body so that she could look up at me, the tears had fallen.

"I love you too."

I waited for her to say, 'but' and give a reason she couldn't anymore, and I wouldn't have blamed her after all she'd been through. Hell, with what I put her through.

Instead, Harlow stood on her tiptoes and brought my face down to hers so that we could kiss.

The burden that I'd been holding on to felt lighter after pouring my heart out to Harlow. I enjoyed being like this with her and the allure of staying here forever was there, but we needed to head back to New York City, and I needed to find Falcone.

He'd still been keeping a low profile, much to the dismay of both Kingston and me. There was some talk on the street that he might be dead, but I doubted it. Until we could prove he was beyond a reasonable doubt, I was operating under the assumption that he was alive and well, waiting for his turn to strike.

It didn't matter what he did now or what deep connections he had. Falcone was a dead man

24

HARLOW

"You can quit glaring at him now."

"I don't know what you're talking about."

I rolled my eyes at Ace. He was the one who brought up me taking self-defense classes, but now he had something against the guy who was instructing me.

"I'm sure you don't. I need to grab a couple of things and then we can head out. How about you show Clark to the door and by the time you're done, we can be on our way?"

Before Ace could disagree with me, I walked over to Clark and shook his hand. "Thanks so much for coming out here. We'll see each other next week."

I spun on my heel and left the living room because I was too excited. I'd deal with Ace's jealousy over Clark being close to me later, but for now, I focused my attention on going to Beyond the Page.

After I'd grabbed my bag and a coat from the closet, I met Ace downstairs in the foyer and together, we drove to Brentson.

"HOW MANY BOOKS does one person need?"

I glared at Ace. "Did you really just ask me that?"

"That was out of curiosity more than anything."

I snorted and shook my head. Ace wouldn't admit that he'd misspoken, especially when it came to me and my books. "Infinity. How could someone ask such a question?"

Although I muttered the last sentence under my breath, Ace heard me and chuckled. I placed another book in the shopping basket and continued shopping, with Ace following behind me.

"You know, for someone who gets plenty of action because of me reading some of these books, you have some nerve to complain."

"Oh, I'm not complaining at all. I was stating a fact and what you forgot to mention, sweetness, is that I can get you hot and bothered damn well on my own."

I didn't have a response. Instead, I felt my cheeks warm slightly and I walked away from him to cool down. Because of course he was right.

"Okay, I'm done!" I announced sometime later and turned to find Ace, who had been carrying the shopping basket around for me. I filled the basket to the brim with books that I couldn't wait to dig into. It was comical to see Ace carrying around this basket for me, given how our relationship started out. But here we were.

I thought it would be weird having Ace following me around the store, but it wasn't. Having him here had been different yet fun, but I knew he still had some things to do to prepare for his meeting, so I hadn't been expecting him to take time out of his day to accompany me to a bookstore.

When we were a couple of feet away from the cash register, Chanel looked up and smiled at Ace and me.

"Good afternoon," she said. "Looks like you have several weeks of reading ahead of you, Harlow."

"She'll finish these books in less than a week," he said as he set the basket down on the counter.

Once I saw my books were safely in a place they couldn't be harmed, I elbowed him in the gut, and he laughed.

We happily chatted with Chanel about our day and the books I was buying, and things just felt... normal. It was as if we were a happy couple in love, enjoying a quiet afternoon at a bookshop.

In love...

My gaze drifted over to Ace, and I caught him staring at me. Did Ace know how to love? Hell, did I?

I watched as his eyes drifted across my entire face, studying me as if no one else in the world mattered. When his brown eyes turned a shade darker, I knew what he was thinking about. That was something that shouldn't be done in public.

The claim he had over me was scary. Leaving him had been one of the hardest things I'd ever done and now that I was back to being his, I still fought to keep my guard up because, deep down, the question of when this would end was still there.

Ace must have noticed something was amiss because his brow shifted slightly.

"Harlow?"

Chanel's question forced me out of the mood that Ace

and I had created. Before I could hand her my credit card, Ace slid his toward her and stared me down, daring me to argue with him about who was paying for these purchases. I rolled my eyes playfully and grabbed one bag so that Ace wouldn't have to carry the books by himself.

I smiled at the woman in front of me once Ace and I were ready to leave. "It was so great seeing you again, Chanel. We'll see you soon."

"You bet. See you later!"

I walked out of the bookshop after Ace maneuvered his body so that his shoulder was holding the door open for me. While I waited for him to walk through, a piece of paper caught my eye.

A sign hanging up in the window of Beyond the Page was the last push I needed to talk to Ace about this.

I couldn't deny that having a job made me feel good. There was a blanket of independence and security that working created for me, and I missed it. Doing some of the freelance stuff part time while I was in hiding was good because not only did it keep me busy during the day, it gave me a way to earn money. Being back under Ace's roof had changed that dynamic once again. While I could go back to doing more freelance gigs, the opportunity that I just discovered would more than likely be a better fit.

When we were safely in the confines of his car, I said, "I want to get a job and I think I have the perfect one."

Ace opened his mouth to say something but shut it. He leaned back in his seat as he studied me. "Where do you want to work?"

I released a breath I didn't know I'd been holding. It was then I realized that I'd been expecting him to fight me on this. Although his gaze was intense, the nerves I had about all of this shifted.

"I saw a sign outside of Beyond the Page and thought that I could help Chanel out. It'll give me something to do and allow me to be more independent. Not that I'm not grateful for all that you've done, but I want to earn money on my own." My last sentence rushed out as my nerves took over.

"And you're sure you don't want to come and work for me?"

"No. This is something I want to do. For myself."

"If you want to apply, go for it. It's going to take some maneuvering because we need to be mindful of your safety and to be honest, I don't like letting you out of my sight. But we can make it happen because it's something you want to do."

I didn't realize how much having his support meant to me until he said those words. The claim he had over me that I was thinking about earlier? Became an even bigger hold on me and I didn't want him to ever let go.

25

HARLOW

"Well?"

I placed my finger up to my lips, letting Ace know I needed him to be quiet right now because I had my phone up to my ear. I'd been waiting on this call and now it was finally here. It took a split second before I could fully focus my attention on the person on the phone again.

"Harlow, I wanted to offer you a job at Beyond the Page."

It took everything in me to bite back the squeal that threatened to fly out of my mouth. This was something I wanted badly, to get my foot in the door to learn what it might be like to own a bookshop one day and it was finally coming true. I couldn't believe how fortunate I was.

I had to confirm some details with Chanel, including a start date. Once I was off the phone, I turned to Ace with a huge grin that couldn't be contained.

"I knew you would get it."

I pulled back slightly to look Ace in his eyes after our hug. "Oh, yeah?"

"There was no one who was more qualified or driven in that pool of applicants. She had to choose you."

"And you know that because?"

His finger lightly touched my chin before he lifted my face up to look at him. "Because I know you."

He laid a sweet kiss on my lips that would have driven anyone to swoon. Having his lips on mine and being caught in his embrace was the most beautiful thing in the world, something I hoped would never end.

"I did it, Ace. I freaking did it."

A smile brightened his features considerably. "Yes, you did. I'm so proud of you."

"There's something I want to do to celebrate, if you don't mind."

Ace tilted his head slightly and looked at me curiously. "And what is that?"

"I want another night at Elevate."

"You enjoyed the time we spent there, last time, then."

I nodded. "I enjoyed the time I spent there with you."

He brushed my hair back from my face and tucked it behind my ear. "Looks like I'm going to purchase a membership to Elevate for the both of us. Let me call Damien and work this out."

IT WAS a few nights later and once again I was on Ace's arm, walking into the hottest club in town. Ace ended up purchasing memberships for us and once we filled out the proper paperwork and submitted our tests that showed we were both clean, we were both allowed to have some more fun tonight.

The slinky red dress was draped over my body like the designer had made it for me. It caused a surge of confidence that I hadn't felt before. I knew I looked fantastic, and it wasn't just from the stares that I was getting as we walked into Elevate. I also wasn't upset that Ace's possessive side came out. He tucked me into his side with his hand on my waist, showing who I would be going home with tonight. There was no doubt in my mind that Ace would have no problem murdering any man who looked at me wrong.

I palmed the old-fashioned key with a large gold *E* on it before placing it in my purse. It was my ticket to Elevate, and I didn't want to lose it. We walked up to a bar in the main lounge and Ace promptly ordered us drinks. The bartender served us quickly and once Ace paid for them, we walked out of the room and found ourselves in a hallway.

We walked over to a desk and checked several items before we went on our way, exploring what Elevate offered.

When we weren't within hearing distance of anyone else, Ace leaned down to my ear and said, "What's underneath your clothes is for my eyes only because you're fucking mine."

His words sent a tremble through my body that might as well have been an earthquake.

I found myself stopping in front of a room because I couldn't move my eyes. The scene unfolding in front of me had me locked in a trance that I couldn't break. A man and woman were in the middle of fucking each other's brains out and I couldn't look away. The look of pure ecstasy on her face as he drove his cock into her was mesmerizing.

This felt like a private moment between two individuals, but I couldn't look away. Missing any part of this felt sinful but watching it unashamed felt the same.

"Does this scene interest you, sweetness?"

"Yes," I said. My voice sounded foreign to my own ears. It wasn't worth lying to Ace, denying how much this turned me on.

"Good to know. Now we have other matters to attend to."

I swallowed hard. "Are we going to—"

"No. I told you what's underneath your clothes is for me only. I don't share what's mine. Let's go."

Ace wasted no time in pulling me away from the room and leading me down the hallway. After making a left down another hallway, we found another set of rooms and Ace stopped in front of one. I held my breath. Between nerves and excitement, I wasn't sure what would be waiting for me on the other side.

When Ace opened the door, he paused before letting me inside. "You remember your safe word, right?"

I nodded. "Yes, lavender."

"Good girl. Walk inside."

I walked inside and the breath I'd been holding in rushed out. My eyes refused to move from the display in front of me. I expected there to be an enormous bed and have it be the centerpiece of the room. What I didn't expect was for there to be restraints tied to the bed.

I watched over my shoulder as Ace dimmed the lights and I couldn't help but be reminded of when we'd made love in front of the fireplace in Deer Valley.

Ace stepped up behind me and gently kissed my neck, causing goose bumps to form in his wake. I felt his fingertips at the back of my dress, and he soon found what he'd been looking for. He slowly lowered the zipper that kept the piece of fabric from floating to the ground and when it wouldn't move any farther, he pushed the thin straps off of my shoulders and allowed the dress to fall, leaving me in nothing but a black thong. I would have thought that I might be cold because of the lack of clothes I had on, but I was on fire from his touch.

He spun me around so that I was now facing him and kissed me like he hadn't seen me in years. His hands found their way into my hair, anchoring my face to his for as long as he wanted me. When he pulled back, we were both left breathing hard. He grabbed my hand and together we walked over to the bed.

I sat down on the bed and Ace took my face into his hands and left one last thorough kiss on my lips.

"Lie down," he said.

I did as he said, and I couldn't help but watch as he restrained my arms and legs to the bed. I was spread out in front of him, like a feast ready for consumption.

"You don't know how stunning you look. Spread out for me to do whatever I want."

I licked my lips in anticipation and I pulled on my binds. There was no way I was going to get out of this without his help. My eyes landed on Ace again. He made it easy for me not to take my eyes off of him. As he removed the navy suit jacket that he wore here tonight, my eyes were trained on how well the white button shirt he'd worn fit him like a glove, showcasing his muscles that made me wish I could rip the clothing off of him. Then again, my slight movement reminded me that it kept me tied to the bed.

He undid the buttons on the shirt as he studied me, his dark-brown eyes boring into me like he was reading my soul. He did the same as he rid his body of the rest of his clothes and then walked over to the bed.

My gaze lingered on every inch of his body, including the parts of him that were begging for my attention. I couldn't help but wish that he would free me so that I could touch him, but I was still excited to see what he had in store for me.

"You know, I thought about covering those pretty eyes of yours again, but I want you to see everything that I'm going to do to you."

I sighed when he finally made his way onto the bed and the first thing he did was lean forward and kiss me. I took my time savoring the connection we shared with one another until he pulled away.

He wasted no time in finding my breasts, massaging them and licking them, but when he lightly slapped one, I jumped at the sensation, somewhat shocked that he'd done it, but when he quickly replaced his hand with his mouth again, I leaned into his touch, hoping to get more of it.

Then another slap on that breast, which elicited a grunt from his lips. "I love watching your tits bounce up and down."

I couldn't help but wiggle under his touch. Not being able to reach out and touch him felt like torture. When he showed my other breast the same amount of attention, my arousal hit a new level. If my thong wasn't soaked from the escapades we'd watched earlier, it was now. Speaking of my thong, I probably should have taken it off before he strapped me down to the bed.

Ace's hand slid down my body and I gasped when he began playing with the waistband of my thong.

"Is there something you want, sweetness?"

"Yes, and you know what it is."

Ace shook his head and we both knew it was a lie. As he rubbed me through my panties, I bit back a moan and that only encouraged him to add more pressure. "I want to hear the words come from those pretty lips of yours."

This time, it was my turn to smirk. "You want to hear me tell you that I want you to finger my pussy and then fuck me so hard that I forget my name and birthday?"

He adjusted his body so that he was sitting between my outstretched legs. "That's close, but I need to correct you on one thing."

"What's that?"

"This is my pussy."

He tore my thong and tossed the useless piece of fabric over his shoulder. He ran a finger up and down my folds, coating himself in my arousal. My head fell back from all the sensations coursing through my body at top speed. But he continued playing with me like he had all the time in the world and nowhere to go.

I was growing more and more impatient. His teasing was going to be the death of me.

"You're already so soaked, baby."

"Please," I said. I sounded desperate to even my own ears, but I didn't care as long as it got me closer to getting what I wanted. I looked back at him and pulled against the restraints, but all he did was smile.

"That's all you had to say."

And he finally gave me what I wanted. His finger entered me, and it took everything in me not to call out in pleasure.

The wait was over, and he wasted no time giving me exactly what I wanted.

My breathing sped up as he continued to fuck me with his finger without mercy.

"Holy fuck," I screamed out. I could feel my orgasm within reach and when he pulled back, I almost cried.

His loud growl made me realize that he'd finally snapped. With lightning-quick reflexes, he'd had the restraints undone and was situating himself between my legs again. He tapped his dick on my pussy before rubbing himself and then I felt him push his way inside me.

"Oh, my—" My words were cut off when he moved inside of me. I groaned instead.

"That's right, sweetness," he said as he sped up. "You can call out to whoever you want to because nothing is going to stop me from fucking you right now."

It all felt overwhelming and amazing at the same time.

My climax came hard and fast, much like Ace pounding into me. It felt as if all of this was a dream, and it wasn't until Ace found his release that I realized that this was real. This was my reality.

Once he'd cleaned me up, he took his time massaging my wrists and ankles. I knew that we would have to leave soon, but I didn't want to leave. The bubble we created tonight reminded me of the time we spent in Deer Valley, away from the world and ignoring everything that served as a distraction from us.

For the first time in a long time, I could say I was happy. And that thought alone almost made me cry.

26

HARLOW

I took another deep breath, hoping to calm the nerves that threatened to overflow.

"You're going to do an amazing job today, sweetness."

Ace's encouraging words made me smile, taking my mind off of how worried I was about this new experience temporarily. It wasn't hard to believe that I was freaking out over this. Not only did I have the first-day jitters that came with starting a new job, but this could very well be the first step I would take to achieving that dream. It felt as if I was starting a new chapter and a part of me was worried that I was going to fail in this new role.

But what was life without taking a chance? At least with this, this was something that I had more control over.

I'd made it past the hardest part which was applying and interviewing for the job.

"Are you almost ready to go?"

"Yeah."

Ace stepped forward and touched my hand. "Are you sure? You look like you might be sick."

"I'm okay. Just feeling a little antsy. My nerves are getting to me, but I was going to leave in a few minutes, so I'd be a little early for training."

"I'm going to drive you."

That caused me to do a double take. "Wait, why? I thought you'd be busy with work."

"You thought I would miss the opportunity to drive you to your first day at your new job?"

This turn in his tone was at direct odds with the smile on his face. It would have been easy for him to let me drive myself or to have hired someone to take me to work. But he was going out of his way to show that he supported me. That was enough to make me cry if I hadn't fought to hold the tears back. I turned away from Ace before he could see how difficult it was for me to keep it together.

"Do you need anything? We need to grab it quickly if we want to leave ASAP."

I shook my head. "I'm good and ready to go. Thanks."

"Of course."

Once I knew I wouldn't cry, I looked up at Ace and found his warm gaze studying me. "Let's grab your things and head out. I'll also be picking you up from work, too. Maybe we can grab dinner in Brentson, and you can tell me how your first day went?"

"That would be lovely."

Today might be overwhelming and exciting because of me trying to learn my new job, but I also had something to look forward to after the workday was done. I noticed a black

SUV sitting in Ace's driveway, but I waited until we were seated in his Porsche Boxster until I spoke.

"What's with the two men in the black SUV? Are they from Cross Sentinel?"

Ace glanced over his shoulder in the other vehicle's direction before he responded. "Yes, they are. I asked them to help protect you while you are at Beyond the Page."

This was news to me. "Were you planning on telling me this if I hadn't asked?"

I wasn't upset that he'd thought of more provisions to help keep me safe because we discussed that portion of it. What I'd wished he'd done was tell me that this was going to happen instead of having to discover it on my own.

"Yes, but I wanted to wait until we got to Beyond the Page before discussing what measures we would be implementing."

"So that there wouldn't be much of a discussion about it because we would run out of time."

Ace glanced at me before putting the car in drive. "There shouldn't be a discussion at all. I'm doing my best to keep you as safe as I can, and you want to work at Beyond the Page. This is us meeting in the middle here."

I couldn't argue with that. "That's fine. I just wanted you to say something sooner."

Ace shrugged and pulled away from the curb and I stared out the window. A few minutes into our drive, Ace's hand landed on my knee, and I turned to look at it and then at him.

"Your knee was bouncing up and down."

"I hadn't noticed."

Although my knee stopped moving, he didn't remove his hand and I didn't ask him to. His touch comforted me in a way I couldn't explain. I placed my hand on top of his and squeezed. The corner of his lip curved upward, and I couldn't help but smile as well.

When we pulled up in front of Beyond the Page, Ace parked the car and opened the driver's side door. He walked around the car and opened the passenger side door so that I could exit the vehicle as well.

"Have an excellent first day at work, sweetness."

"Thank you."

He leaned forward and his lips grazed mine before he put more intention behind the kiss. And while the kiss wasn't as heated as many of our other ones, I knew it would leave me thinking about it for the rest of the day until we could see each other this evening.

I got out of the car and walked to the front door of Beyond the Page. With a deep breath, I opened the door, and heard what had now become a familiar chime. Chanel looked up from her place behind the front counter. She greeted me with a big smile.

"Welcome to Beyond the Page! That sounds weird to say since you've been here numerous times."

I laughed and some of my nerves calmed. "I'm happy to be here."

"Excellent and I'm so glad that you wanted to join the team. Let me show you where to put your things and we can get started."

"I DIDN'T KNOW what I had been expecting, but I didn't expect to be this tired."

Ace had picked me up after I'd gotten off of work and took me to Bella Vita, a fancy Italian restaurant in Brentson, to celebrate my first day on the job. He'd rented out a private room in the restaurant, though I would have had no issue dining with the rest of Bella Vita's guests. I wasn't going to, but I'd almost asked him if we could do a rain check because I was so tired after a long day, but when he mentioned wine would be involved, I was sold.

"But was your time there fulfilling?"

Ace's question forced me to think about my answer. "It was. I absolutely loved being there and getting a behind-the-scenes look at some things that need to be done to run a bookstore. I love it."

And that was the truth. Chanel took her time showing me how she ran her shop including how she kept track of inventory, how to check out customers, and even a glimpse into how she advertised her business. I was left with my head buzzing with new information, and I couldn't wait to see more of her techniques and ideas in action.

"Good," Ace said before lifting his glass up to his lips.

"And how was your day?"

"Not as exciting as yours. Putting the finishing touches on what I'm presenting to the board of directors."

"That must be stressful." On top of everything else he was balancing he still had a company to run. I watched as his expression darkened. What had caused it?

"It has its moments."

"Are there a bunch of assholes on your company's board?"

He smirked for a moment before the storminess in his eyes returned. At least I got a positive response out of him for a second.

"You could say that, although it's more complicated."

Now I was thankful that we were in a private room. Having these moments where Ace opened up to me was special because he kept thoughts about himself, and his backstory guarded.

"Please continue," I said.

"But you should tell me more about how your day has gone. After all, that is why we're celebrating."

"It's okay for us to talk about you, too. I welcome it. Plus, we don't have anywhere to be anytime soon, Ace. What has you stressed out about this meeting?"

"My grandfather is still on the board, so he'll be attending the meeting virtually."

That was when it all clicked. Everything that he told me made sense.

I leaned forward even though he and I were the only people in the room and said, "Based on what you told me about him, I would assume he's probably using this to exert control over you."

"You'd be right."

I shook my head. "That's so fucked up."

"I mean, compared to your childhood—"

"No." I grabbed his hand and placed it between both of mine. "We aren't comparing childhood traumas. We've both seen and had to deal with a lot, but that doesn't make my struggle any harder than yours. They're incomparable."

His stare bore into me as if he was peeling every layer back to get to my soul. He stood up from his seat quickly and I gasped when he kneeled in front of me and pulled my face to his. Before our lips touched, I felt this force pulling us together and the only thing either of us could do was give in.

When he nibbled on my lip before kissing me again, I groaned. Now I really wished we'd just gone straight home.

Someone cleared their throat and I jumped slightly. We weren't alone anymore. I turned my head and found our waiter standing there. I hadn't heard him open the door and enter the room. Out of the corner of my eye, I saw Ace stand up.

"Is there something I can help you with?"

I licked my lips to keep my composure because Ace was not happy with the interruption.

"I-I'm sorry for disturbing you. Can I take your orders for dinner?"

I could feel the warmth spreading through my cheeks. I turned to look at Ace, who was walking back over to his seat across from me. Once he sat down, I picked up my menu, determined to figure out what I wanted to eat instead of begging Ace to kiss me again.

27

ACE

I typed up an email on my computer while another conference call droned on. Working from home had become the norm for me since Harlow was back in my home and traveling to and from the city had become more taxing on the time I wished to spend with her. Being able to leave work behind at the end of the day and walk upstairs and pull her into my arms was what I craved, not the work I'd used to distract myself with for years as I continued to help my grandfather build up the family company.

I'd put myself on mute so I wouldn't disturb anyone, but I was determined to finish up the things I needed to do because I was leaving here as soon as the board meeting was over. Spending more time with Harlow was a priority, which was why I outsourced the digging into where the hell Falcone was to Cross Sentinel.

You would think that the killing of one of his men would have been enough to bring him out of whatever hole he'd crawled into, but he hadn't resurfaced and the search for him continued.

Harlow was busy with her new job at Beyond the Page. But most importantly, she was happy.

Things were going well considerably, and things between Harlow and me were better than ever.

A knock on the door shook me from my thoughts of Harlow.

"Mr. Bolton?"

"Yes."

"It's time to head down to the conference room to prepare for the board meeting."

"Very well. Thanks, Helen."

I wanted to get down to the conference room early to make sure that everything was ready to go myself. While my team here was fantastic, having a quick run-through before the board arrived would calm some of the tension buzzing around the office. Or maybe that was just within me.

With my team gathered around the conference table, we did a quick run-through to make sure that everything looked good for the presentations that were to start in about fifteen minutes.

I adjusted my tie and pulled down the sleeves of my suit jacket. It was game time.

I sat down at the head of the table and watched as my team made their speeches. The applause that each person received at the end of their presentations was well warranted because of the superb jobs they'd done. I watched each director's face and almost all of them seemed to be pleased except one: my grandfather.

When I took over as CEO, I'd made a vow to improve on what he'd done and change what wasn't working. It was obvious that he wasn't happy with some changes I'd made. That was his problem, not mine.

When it was my turn to begin, I stood up and caught my grandfather's eye. I could see that he was going to challenge me when I opened the floor up for questioning and I looked forward to it.

"I HAVE a question about your idea for expanding our reach in the Southwest."

It took everything in me to not grip the edge of the table and show him what I really thought about his question. Keeping a professional front was of utmost importance, especially in front of my company's directors, even if it meant doing everything in my power not to lose my shit in front of my grandfather.

He was the one who stepped down as CEO to join the board.

He was the one who handed the reins over to me.

And now he was doing everything he could to show me up, to make me look incompetent in a room filled with his peers. Didn't he realize it also reflected poorly on him, since he was the one who chose me to be his successor?

"The answer to this was mentioned on a previous slide. But there seems to be ample opportunity for expanding our outreach out there based on the research we've done and the interviews we have. Several companies have expressed interest in having us buy them, which could be a good starting point as well. We are exploring all of our options. Are there any more questions?"

My grandfather became slightly flustered at my dismissal of him, but I couldn't care less. It was time to wrap this meeting up and I'd had enough of his shit. I knew it was a way to get underneath my skin, but I wouldn't allow for him to see the effect it was having on me.

When no one else said a word, I wrapped up the meeting by thanking everyone for coming and assured them that we would see and speak to them again within the coming weeks and at our next meeting.

Several of the board members came up and congratulated me on a well-done meeting and it didn't go unnoticed by me that one person hadn't. I knew it was only a matter of time.

"Ace."

It looked as if that time was now. I took a deep breath and turned to find my grandfather standing behind me. I had to admit he looked well rested, his time on his private island seemed to agree with him.

"I didn't expect you to show up in person." My grandfather had taken to attending board meetings virtually because he didn't feel like traveling. It had been a few years since I'd last been in the same room as him.

"I wanted to surprise you. You handled yourself well up there."

"You didn't seem to want to make it any easier." I couldn't resist the jab.

"I just had a few questions, that's all. Do you have some time to get a drink or two?"

What I saw on the documents Parker gave me floated to the surface and the temptation to ask about Kiki Hastings was there. But I didn't because we were in public. In fact, the last thing I wanted to do was spend more time with him. "I have plans tonight."

"Well, I'll be in town for the next few days if you can find the time to meet with me."

"Sure. I'll send you a text."

I didn't bother saying goodbye because I knew it would only cause further aggravation for both of us. After reaching my office, I packed my bag and went down to the lobby.

As I stepped into the waiting vehicle, I loosened my tie. Now that it was over, I couldn't wait to get back and see Harlow. I planned on having my driver drop me off at Beyond the Page and together we could ride back home and have a nice, cozy dinner for two.

Home.

The dark, vast dungeon of a place didn't feel like a death sentence with her in it. Now that I had the board meeting off my back, I knew what I needed to conquer next: doing more to find Falcone and talking to Harlow about what changes we needed to make so she felt more comfortable in my life. I'd bought the condo for us in New York City because it was something she'd loved. It was far past time to meld our lives together, and I was ready to do just that. No more games, no more second-guessing anything, especially when it came to us.

When I saw the doubt in her eyes, I tried my best to soothe the troubled expression from her face, but none of my efforts had worked because it had taken me time to get to the mental space to offer her more. My confession when we were in Deer Valley was something, but it wasn't enough.

All of that ended tonight.

28

HARLOW

I hummed to myself in the back room as I grabbed some books that I could use to restock the shelves at Beyond the Page.

Work over the last couple of weeks had been wonderful. Being able to get out of the house and earn a living had done great things for my mental health. The transition had been easy so far, and I'd already learned so much from Chanel. I was soaking up as much information as possible.

That was still the overarching goal, but I was treating my job at Beyond the Page as an apprenticeship. Some evenings, I would return home and find Ace in his office, where I would tell him everything about my day. Other evenings, Ace would be the one who would pick me up, and he and I would talk about our respective days at work. I couldn't wait to get home and stay in bed with him for most of the weekend.

When my phone vibrated in my pocket, I pulled it out, happy to see a text message from Ace.

Ace: *Just left my office, so I should be there by the time you get off of work. How about a quiet evening at home tonight?*

Me: *That sounds amazing. Can't wait. See you soon!*

I stuffed my phone back into my pocket. Suddenly, I heard the door to the room slam open. I jumped slightly but didn't turn around. It could be Chanel coming to the back to grab something.

The hairs on the back of my neck were standing at attention. After everything that happened between Ian's murder and Falcone being on the run, I was on high alert. But there was supposed to be someone watching over Beyond the Page when I had a shift. That didn't ease the fear I was feeling. I grabbed a heavy book and swung around, prepared to throw it even if it would hurt me to damage this book. I was shocked to find Emma standing there.

"Emma! What the hell happened to you?"

Her appearance was disheveled, her brown hair everywhere. The bags under her eyes indicated she hadn't gotten much sleep recently.

"Nothing," she said, shaking her head. "Nothing happened to me."

"That's a lie. You haven't called me in weeks!"

Her gaze narrowed considerably. "Not everything is about you, Harlow."

The snappiness in her voice made me jerk my head back. Ace's warning about her rang in my mind, all signs pointing to something not being right. I didn't know what kind of state she was in, so I didn't want to upset her. "I didn't intend for that to come out that way. I was worried about you, but I'm glad to see that you're okay."

"Am I really okay?"

I took a step back from her. Her response to my question was odd. I didn't know what I was dealing with here.

"What happened to you? Why didn't you call?" The words rushed out of my mouth without me thinking. How had she managed to get into the back room of Beyond the Page?

"Things were keeping me... preoccupied. I had some business to take care of." Her voice was terse, and I took another step away from her. Something was clearly wrong, and I didn't know what had gotten into her. My gut told me I needed to get out of this situation and fast.

"Is there something you need?"

I reached into my back pocket to see if I could trigger the alarm on my phone to send out an SOS signal for help.

"Stop moving, Harlow." Her eyes moved from me and haphazardly jumped around the room, landing anywhere and everywhere as if she was searching for something. How they were darting around made me wonder how she could focus long enough in order to find whatever she was looking for.

I'd gone into the back to grab a few books and should have made it back out to the front of the store within a couple of minutes. Why hadn't anyone come to check on me?

Wasn't there supposed to be a team of people watching me in case something like this happened? I stepped back when I noticed a sadistic smile crossing her lips. She held a gun up to my face and my hands flew up to show that I had nothing that could hurt her.

"You're going to come with me. You and I have somewhere that we need to go."

How had she made it past the security detail that was supposed to be watching this place?

"I'm not coming with you anywhere. We can sit down and

talk about this because we are friends, remember? Please put the gun away."

How I managed to say that calmly, I'll never know.

"Nice try, Harlow. Let's go. Turn around and walk over to the door so that we can leave the building."

I went through some of the self-defense moves I'd learned but was afraid to try them. There was no way I could compete with someone holding a gun in my face, so I followed her directions. I noticed she seemed to have a good feel for the layout of the bookstore, which meant that she'd probably been stalking me and this place for quite some time.

I needed to think fast. There had to be a way that I could get away from her and get to safety. The likelihood of me finding something to use to distract Emma was fading fast and when my eyes landed on some cardboard boxes by the last door that would lead us into the alleyway behind Beyond the Page, I knew what I had to do. I had to take this chance and if I was going to die trying, well, so be it.

I love you, Ace.

I held back the emotions so that it didn't raise any suspicions with Emma before I acted. Everything happened within a split second. As I paused briefly to open the back door, I held the door open with my foot and there was just enough space between me and Emma that allowed me to yank the stacked boxes down and behind me, allowing me to cause enough confusion so that she didn't know what to do. Before I could see if my plan had worked, I took off running.

While I'd never been the best at running, swimming laps in Ace's pool must have helped my stamina because I was able to get around through the back alleyway and to the street within seconds. Part of me wanted to run back into the bookstore and have Chanel call the police, but I didn't want to run the risk that Emma might not give a damn about who she killed in the process of getting me and risk getting Chanel killed. Instead, I grabbed my keys from my pocket and hopped into the car I'd driven to work today.

I hurried up and locked the car doors and started the vehicle. When I looked around to see if I saw the black SUV that had been parked at Ace's house this morning, I saw Emma had made her way out of the back alley and was staring right at me. That was all it took for me to put the car into drive and pull out of the parking space.

My heart was beating loudly in my ears as I raced down the street. Where I was going, I had no idea.

I managed to use the Bluetooth in my car to dial Ace's phone number.

"Please pick up the phone, Ace. Please pick up the phone."

The ringing on the other end of the phone felt as if it had been going on for centuries until I heard a familiar voice filter through the car's speakers.

"Hello, sweetness."

"Ace." My voice was shaky. I was acting on autopilot, driving to who the hell knew where.

"What's wrong?" His tone changed from slightly teasing to concerned in a hot minute.

"I'm currently driving the BMW through Brentson," I said. "Emma is chasing me. Please, I need your help now." I paused and looked in my rearview mirror, hoping that I'd see a police car. Instead, I saw a black sedan that was gaining on me. Was it Emma, and if so, how had she caught up so quickly?

"Fuck! I'm still a ways out. Where the hell are Kingston's men?" Ace almost shouted in my ear as anger pulsated through his voice.

"I don't know, and I'm scared. I'm so damn scared."

"I know, baby. Everything is going to be fine."

Ace said something to someone else in the background, but my brain couldn't process what he was saying.

"They're gaining on me!" I was shaking now, barely able to keep a grip on the wheel due to how sweaty my hands had become.

"Try to remain calm. I just got word that another team from Cross Sentinel is in route and that they aren't that far away. I need you to hold on, baby, okay? Help is on the way."

He sounded about as helpless as I felt right now. I looked in the rearview mirror again, just before the black sedan behind me tapped my back bumper.

"They just hit the back of my car. They're trying to make me crash!"

I thought about Emma having a gun and that it was only a matter of time before they started shooting. I looked back again to see if there was a way that I could avoid what they might have planned next, but when I looked back through my windshield, it was too late.

Everything seemed to slow down. As I saw what was about to happen, I felt the scream leave my throat. There was nothing I could do to prevent the crash. I could hear Ace saying something, but what it was, I had no idea.

Within seconds, everything went black.

THANK YOU FOR READING! The next book in the series, The Billionaire's Vengeance, will be released in Summer 2022.

WANT to join the discussion about the The Ruthless Billionaire Trilogy? Click HERE to join my Reader Group on Facebook.

PLEASE JOIN my newsletter to find out the latest about the The Ruthless Billionaire Trilogy and my other books!

ABOUT THE AUTHOR

Bri loves a good romance, especially ones that involve a hot anti-hero. That is why she likes to turn the dial up a notch with her own writing. Her Broken Cross series is her debut dark romance series.

She spends most of her time hanging out with her family, plotting her next novel, or reading books by other romance authors.

briblackwood.com

ALSO BY BRI BLACKWOOD

Broken Cross Series

Sinners Empire (Prequel)

Savage Empire

Scarred Empire

Steel Empire

Shadow Empire

Secret Empire

Stolen Empire

The Broken Cross Series Box Set: Books 1-3

The Ruthless Billionaire Trilogy

The Billionaire's Auction

The Billionaire's Possession

The Billionaire's Vengeance

Brentson University Series

Devious Game